# *The Personal Touch*

---

*J. Wilbur Chapman*

# Contents

# THE PERSONAL TOUCH

BY

J. Wilbur Chapman

## *FOREWORD*

IF

If to be a Christian is worth while, then the most ordinary interest in those with whom we come in contact should prompt us to speak to them of Christ.

*　　*　　*　　*　　*

If the New Testament be true--and we know that it is--who has given us the right to place the responsibility for soul-winning on other shoulders than our own?

*　　*　　*　　*　　*

If they who reject Christ are in danger, is it not strange that we, who are so sympathetic when the difficulties are physical or temporal, should apparently be so devoid of interest as to allow our friends and neighbours and kindred to come into our lives and pass out again without a word of invitation to accept Christ, to say nothing of sounding a note of warning because of their peril?

*　　*　　*　　*　　*

If to-day is the day of salvation, if to-morrow may never come, and if life is equally uncertain, how can we eat, drink, and be merry when those who live with us, work with us, walk with us, and love us are unprepared for eternity because they are unprepared for time?

*　　*　　*　　*　　*

If Jesus called His disciples to be fishers of men, who gave us the right to be satisfied with making fishing tackle or pointing the way to the fishing banks instead of going ourselves to cast out the net until it be filled?

*　　*　　*　　*　　*

If Jesus Himself went seeking the lost, if Paul the Apostle was in agony because his kinsmen, according to the flesh, knew not Christ, why should we not consider it worth while to go out after the lost until they are found?

\*      \*      \*      \*      \*

If I am to stand at the judgment seat of Christ to render an account for the deeds done in the body, what shall I say to Him if my children are missing, my friends not saved, or if my employer or employee should miss the way because I have been faithless?

\*      \*      \*      \*      \*

If I wish to be approved at the last, then let me remember that no intellectual superiority, no eloquence in preaching, no absorption in business, no shrinking temperament, no spirit of timidity can take the place of or be an excuse for my not making an honest, sincere, prayerful effort to win others to Christ by means of the *Personal Touch*.

# CHAPTER I
## *A Testimony*

I have the very best of reasons for believing in the power of the personal touch in Christian work, especially as it may be used in the winning of others to Christ.

My boyhood's home was in the city of Richmond, in the State of Indiana, my mother was a devout member of the Methodist Episcopal Church, and in the first years of my life in company with my father and the other children of the household, I attended the church of my mother. When she was just a little more than thirty-five years of age she was called home. My father in his youth had been trained as a Presbyterian; many of his ancestors having belonged to that denomination; therefore it was quite natural that he should return to the Church of his fathers when my mother had gone home.

It was thus I became a member of the Presbyterian Church, and my Church training as a boy after fifteen years of age was in that denomination. Because of this special interest in both the Church of my father and my mother, I attended two Sunday Schools. In the morning I was in a class in the Presbyterian school and in the afternoon was a member of a class in the Grace Methodist Sunday School, my teacher in the afternoon school being Mrs C.C. Binckley, a godly woman, the wife of Senator Binckley of Indiana, through all her life from girlhood, a devout follower of Christ and a faithful teacher in the Sunday School. Not so very long ago I heard that she was still teaching in the same school, and I am sure, as in the olden days, winning boys to Christ.

I fear that I was a thoughtless boy, and yet the impressions made upon my life in those days by the death of my mother, the teaching of my father, and the influence of my Sunday School teacher, were such that I have never been able to get away from them.

One Sunday afternoon a stranger came to address our school--his name I have never learned; I would give much to find it out. At the close of his address he made an appeal to the scholars to stand and confess Christ. I think every boy in my class rose to his feet with the exception of myself. I found myself reasoning thus: Why should I rise, my mother was a saint; my father is one of the truest men I know; my home teaching has been all that a boy could have; I know about Christ and think I realise His power to save.

While I was thus reasoning, my Sunday School teacher, with tears in her eyes, leaned around back of the other boys and looking straight at me, as I turned towards her she said, "Would it not be best for you to rise?" And when she saw that I still hesitated, she put her hand under my elbow and lifted me just a little bit, and I stood upon my feet. I can never describe my emotions. I do not know that that was the time of my conversion, but I do know that it was the day when one of the most profound impressions of my life was made upon me. Through all these years I have never forgotten it, and it was my Sunday School teacher who influenced me thus to take the stand--it was her personal touch that gave me courage to rise before the school and confess my Saviour.

In the good providence of God, during my student days, as well as during the first years of my ministry, I was thrown in contact with men who knew God, who were being marvellously used by Him, and who seemed ready and willing to give assistance to one who was just beginning the journey of life with all its struggles and conflicts ahead of him.

When I was a student attending Lake Forest University, not far from Chicago, I was very greatly troubled about the matter of assurance. I heard that Mr Moody was to be in Chicago, and in company with a friend I went in from Lake Forest to hear him. Five times in a single day I sat at his feet and drank in the words which fell from his lips. He thrilled me through and through. I heard him preach his great sermon on "Sowing and Reaping," when old Farwell Hall was crowded with young men many of whom were students like myself.

The impression that Mr Moody made upon me as a Christian young man, was that I myself was not absolutely sure I was saved. I analysed my experience and found that sometimes I was more than sure and at other times dwelt in Doubting Castle. When the great evangelist called for an after-meeting, I was one of the first to enter the room where he had indicated he would meet those who were interested, and to my great joy he came and sat down beside me. He asked me my difficulty and I told him I was not quite sure that I was saved. He asked me to read John v. 24, and trembling with emotion I read: "Verily, verily, I say unto you, He that heareth my word, and believeth on Him that sent me, hath everlasting life, and shall not come into condemnation; but is passed from death unto life."

He said to me, "Do you believe this?" I said, "Certainly." He said, "Are you a Christian?" and I replied, "Sometimes I think I am, and again I am fearful." Then he said, "Read it again." And I read it once more. His question was again repeated, and I answered it in the same manner as before. Then he seemed to lose his patience, and the only time I can remember Mr Moody being sharp with me was when he turned upon me and said, "Whom are you doubting?" And suddenly it dawned upon me that I was doubting Him who said I was possessed of everlasting life because I believed on the Son and on the Father who had sent Him, and in spite of this possession and His sure Word of promise concerning it, I was sceptical. But as I sat there beside him I saw it all. Then he said, "Read it again." And I read it the third time, and talking to me as gently as a mother would to her child he said, "Do you believe this?" I said, "Yes, indeed I do." Then he said, "Are you a Christian?" And I answered, "Yes, Mr Moody, I am." From that day to this I have never questioned my acceptance with God.

For some reason Mr Moody always seemed to keep me in mind. He came into my church in the early days of my ministry, told me where he thought I was wrong and suggested how I might be more greatly used of God. He advised me to give my time wholly to evangelistic work, and when I said to him one day that I was going to take up the pastorate after three years of experience in general evangelism, he seemed disturbed. To him more than to any other man, I owe the greatest blessing that ever came into my life.

Through Mr Moody I met the Rev F.B. Meyer, and one sentence which he used at Northfield changed my ministry. He said, "If you are not willing to give up everything for Christ, are you willing to be made willing?" That seemed like a new star in the sky of my life, and one day acting upon his suggestion, after having carefully studied the passages in the New Testament which relate to surrender and to consecration, I gave myself anew to Christ and I shall never be able to express in words my appreciation of what this man of God to whom I have referred, did for me by personal influence.

All along the way I have been brought in contact with men whom God has signally blessed, and I am persuaded that there are many to-day whose hearts are hungering for a blessing, who are waiting as I was myself, for someone to speak to them personally, and help them out of darkness into light; out of a certain kind of bondage into a glorious freedom. The personal touch in Christian work, to me, means everything.

# CHAPTER II
## *A General Principle*

I have been amazed in my study of the biographies of men and women who have been specially used of God, to see how almost universal is the rule that they have come to Christ, or to an experience of power, through the personal influence of a friend or acquaintance. Preaching is not enough, it is sometimes too general; the impressions of a song may soon be effaced, but the personal touch, the tear in the eye, the pathos in the voice, the concern which is manifested in the very expression of one's countenance; these are used with great effect, and thousands of people are to-day in the Kingdom of God, or in special service, because of such influences being brought to bear upon their lives.

John Wesley is a notable illustration of the influence of the personal touch. Peter Bohler of the Moravian Church, came into his life when he was in sore need of just such assistance as he seemed able to give. Dr W. H. Fitchett of Australia, writes:--

"The Moravians of Savannah taught him exactly what Peter Bohler taught him afterwards in London, but the teaching at the moment left his life unaffected. Wesley's own explanation is, 'I understood it not; I was too learned and too wise, so that it seemed foolishness unto me; and I continued preaching, and following after, and trusting in that righteousness whereby no flesh can be justified.'

"The truth is that Peter Bohler himself, had he met Wesley in Savannah, would have taught him in vain. The stubborn Sacramentarian and High Churchman had to be scourged, by the sharp discipline of failure, out of that subtlest and deadliest form of pride, the pride that imagines that the secret of salvation lies, or can lie, within the circle of purely human effort. Wesley later describes Peter Bohler as 'One whom God prepared for me.' But God in the toilsome and humiliating experiences of Georgia, was preparing Wesley for Peter Bohler."

Bohler described Wesley as "a man of good principles, who did not properly believe on the Saviour, and was willing to be taught." Later on, in the city of London, where Wesley had been intimately associated with Peter Bohler and had come directly under his influence, he one night attended a religious service in Aldersgate Street, where the one conducting the service was reading Luther's preface to the Epistle to the Romans. The effect of that service upon Wesley is best told in his own words.

"About a quarter before nine, while he was describing the change which God works in the heart through faith in Christ, I felt my heart strangely warmed. I felt I did trust in Christ, Christ alone, for my salvation; and an assurance was given me that He had taken away my sins, even mine, and saved me from the law of sin and death. I began to pray with all my might for those who had in a more special manner despitefully used me and persecuted me. I then testified openly to all there what I now first felt in my heart. But it was not long before the enemy suggested, 'This cannot be faith; for where is thy joy?' Then was I taught that peace and victory over sin are essential to faith in the Captain of our salvation; but that, as to the transports of joy that usually attend the beginning of it, especially in those who have mourned deeply, God sometimes giveth, sometimes withholdeth, them according to the counsels of His own will."

Charles Haddon Spurgeon, in speaking of his own early experiences, writes thus: "When I was a young child staying with my grandfather, there came to preach in the village Mr Knill, who had been a missionary at St Petersburgh, and a mighty preacher of the gospel. He came to preach for the London Missionary Society, and arrived on the Saturday at the manse. He was a great soul winner, and he soon spied out the boy. He said to me, 'where do you sleep? for I want to call you up in the morning.' I showed him my little room. At six o'clock he called me up, and we went into the arbour. There, in the sweetest way, he told me of the love of Jesus and of the blessedness of trusting in Him and loving Him in our childhood. With many a story he preached Christ to me, and told me how good God had been to him, and then he prayed that I might know the Lord and serve Him.

"He knelt down in the arbour and prayed for me with his arms about my neck. He did not seem content unless I kept with him in the interval between the services, and he heard my childish talk with patient love. On Monday morning he did as on the Sabbath, and again on Tuesday. Three times he taught me and prayed with me, and before he had to leave, my grandfather had come back from the place where he had gone to preach, and all the family were gathered to morning prayer. Then, in the presence of them all, Mr Knill took me on his knee and said, 'This child will one day preach the gospel, and he will preach it to great multitudes. I am persuaded that he will preach in the chapel of Rowland Hill, where (I think he said) I am now the minister.' He spoke very solemnly, and called upon all present to witness what he said."

D.L. Moody was thus won to Christ. His Sunday School teacher in Boston was Mr E.D. Kimball. He was not one of the ordinary type of Sunday School teachers. Mere literal instruction on Sunday did not satisfy his ideal of the teacher's duty. He knew his boys, and if he knew them, it was because he studied them, because he became acquainted with their occupations and aims, visiting them during the week. It was his custom, moreover, to find opportunity to give to his boys an opportunity to use his experience in seeking the better things of the Spirit. The day came when he resolved to speak to young Moody about Christ, and about his soul.

"I started down to Holton's shoe store," says Mr Kimball. "When I was nearly there, I began to wonder whether I ought to go just then, during business hours. And I thought maybe my mission might embarrass the boy, that when I went away the other clerks might ask who I was, and when they learned might taunt Moody and ask if I was trying to make a good boy out of him. While I was pondering over it all, I passed the store without noticing it. Then when I found I had gone by the door, I determined to make a dash for it and have it over at once. I found Moody in the back part of the store wrapping up shoes in paper and putting them on shelves. I went up to him and put my hand on his shoulder, and as I leaned over I placed my foot upon a shoe box. Then I made my plea, and I feel that it was really a very weak one. I don't know just what words I used, nor could Mr Moody tell. I simply told him of Christ's love for him and the love Christ wanted in return. That was all there was of it. I think Mr Moody said afterwards that there were tears in my eyes. It seemed that the young man was just ready for the light that then broke upon him, for there at once in the back of that shoe store in Boston the future great evangelist gave himself and his life to Christ."

Many years afterward Mr Moody himself told the story of that day. "When I was in Boston," he said, "I used to attend a Sunday School class, and one day, I recollect, my teacher came around behind the counter of the shop I was at work in, and put his hand upon my shoulder, and talked to me about Christ and my soul. I had not felt that I had a soul till then. I said to myself. This is a very strange thing. Here is a man who never saw me till lately, and he is weeping over my sins, and I never shed a tear about them. But, I understand it now, and know what it is to have a passion for men's souls and weep over their sins. I don't remember what he said, but I can feel the power of that man's hand on my shoulder to-night. It was not long after that I was brought into the Kingdom of God."

The personal touch is necessary. It is not so much what we say, as the way we say it, and indeed, it is not so much what we say and the way we say it, as what we are, that counts in personal work. We cannot delegate this work to others. God has called the evangelist to a certain mission in soul winning. He has given ministers the privilege of winning many to Christ. Mission workers, generally, are charged with the responsibility for this special work. But this fact cannot relieve the parents, the children, the husband, the wife, the friends, the business man, the toiler in the shop, from personal responsibility in the matter of attempting to win others to the Saviour.

# CHAPTER III
## *A Polished Shaft*

"He hath made me a polished shaft; in his quiver hath he hid me," Isaiah xlix. 2.[1] Personal preparation is essential to the best success in personal work. No familiarity with the methods of other workers; no distinction among men because of past favours of either God or men; no past success in the line of special effort; no amount of intellectual equipment and no reputation for cleverness in the estimation of your fellowmen will take the place of individual soul culture, if you are to be used of God.

Thou must be true thyself,
If thou the truth would teach;
It takes the overflow of heart
To give the lips full speech.

The words of Isaiah the Prophet literally refer to Him who was the servant of Jehovah. He was God's prepared blessing to a waiting and needy people. He came from the bosom of the Father that He might lift a lost and ruined race to God. And swifter than an arrow speeds from the hand of the archer when the string of the bow is drawn back, He came to do the will of God. In the Epistle to the Hebrews we find Him saying, "Lo I come, in the volume of the Book it is written of me I delight to do thy will." This was the spirit of all His earthly life. When He was hungry and sent His disciples to buy meat, He found it unnecessary to partake of the food they brought to Him, saying, "My meat is to do the will of him that sent me." And when He came to the garden of Gethsemane, well on to the climax of His sacrificial life, we hear Him saying again, "Not my will, but Thine be done." In such a completely surrendered life we have a perfect representation of the prepared Christian worker.

In the expression of Isaiah we have also the thought of His anguish. "He was

---

1 Suggested by Dr Charles Cuthbert Hall.

made a polished shaft." In these days when there is a disposition to place Jesus upon the level with others who have wrought for the good of humanity, it is well to remember that He is the Lamb slain from the foundation of the world. There is also the thought of the beauty of His character, for He is a "polished shaft," "chiefest among ten thousand," and "the One altogether lovely." He is "the lily of the valley" for fragrance, and "the rose of Sharon" for beauty, and thus prepared He stands before us beckoning us on to a work which is indescribable in its fascination. Calling His disciples He said, "I will make you fishers of men." The same promise is made to us. Working His miracles He said to those about Him, "Greater works than these shall ye do." We have only to follow in His footsteps and walk sufficiently near to hear His faintest whisper when He directs us to be, in the truest sense of the word, successful personal workers.

It is a great encouragement to hear Him say, "As the Father hath sent me, even so send I you." The shaft mentioned by Isaiah is an arrow prepared with all care. The quiver in which this arrow is placed is carried on the left side of the archer, placed upon the string of the bow, the archer drawing back the string adds to the elasticity of bow and string his own strength, and the shaft is off to do the archer's will. There is in this story an illustration for all Christian workers. Fitness for service lies first of all in divine endowment. God has given to each one of us special and peculiar qualifications. If we live as we ought to live, exercising the gift that is in us; the painter may paint for His glory; the poet may sing and speak of Him; the preacher may preach and declare His righteousness, and should we live in less conspicuous spheres than these, we have only to do our best with that with which He has endowed us and our lives will be pleasing to Him.

It lies also in the divine call. The shaft was made for a special purpose. We have been created to do His will. The possession of power is not enough; talents unused will rise at the Judgment Seat to rebuke us. God gives us ability and then calls us forth into the field that we may exercise it. Fitness for service also lies in the response to God's will. The possession of power and the call of God may both be realised and we may still fail. It is when we say "I will," to God that human weakness is linked to divine strength and then a great service is possible.

Life is not drudgery, it is an inspiration.

"Let me but do my work from day to day,
In field or forest, at desk or loom;
When vagrant wishes beckon me away,
Let me but find it in my heart to say,
This is my work, my blessing not my doom;
Of all who live I am the only one by whom
This work can best be done."

The word of the Prophet Isaiah is a picture of the child of God, as well as of Him who is our inspiration for service. There is the thought of definiteness of use in the shaft. Other articles may be created for a variety of purposes. This shaft is made to go at the owner's will. There is only one way to live in this world and that is according to the will of God and for His glory.

It matters little where I was born,
Or if my parents were rich or poor;
Whether they shrank from the cold world's scorn,
Or walked in the pride of wealth secure;
But whether I live a surrendered man,
And hold my integrity firm in my clutch,
I tell you, my brother, as plain as I can,
It matters much!

It matters little where be my grave,
Or on the land or on the sea.
By purling brook, or 'neath stormy wave,
It matters little or nought to me;
But whether the angel of death comes down
And marks my brow with his loving touch,
And one that shall wear the victor's crown,
It matters much!

There is also in this picture of the shaft the thought of directed motion. The aim is everything. The arrow cannot aim itself. There is no such thing as an aimless life. Our energies are either being directed for Christ or against Him; in the interests of humanity or contrary to them. Every child of God must reach the place where he will say, Not my will, but Thine, O God, be done; not my path but Thine, O Christ, be travelled; not my ambitions realized but Thine own purposes in me fulfilled, my Heavenly Father. The progress of such a life is peace, the consummation of it the most perfect victory.

When I am dying how glad I shall be
That the lamp of my life has been blazed out for Thee.
I shall be glad in whatever I gave,
Labour, or money, one sinner to save;
  I shall not mind that the path has been rough,
That Thy dear feet led the way is enough.
When I am dying how glad I shall be,
That the lamp of my life has been blazed out for Thee.

In the picture of the archer and his arrow, there is an illustration of derived energy. The arrow placed upon the string and drawn back by the archer speeds away to do the master's will. It has no power in itself; it flies forward in the master's strength. God is always seeking an outlet for His power along the line of service. It is when our lives are surrendered to Him that victory is possible. A friend of mine took for his year text the expression "I believe, and I belong." We might well add, "I live and I love," and because I do both I will obey. Ole Bull once played his violin in the presence of a company of University students. He charmed them, they knew at once that they were in the presence of a master. When he was finished playing, one who was present said to him, "What is the secret of your power, have you a special bow, or is it in the instrument you use?" Ole Bull responded, "I think it is in neither, but it has always seemed to me that I had power in playing because I waited to play until I had an inspiration, when my soul was overflowing with music and I could not stay the torrent that was back of me; it is then that I take my violin and the music flows forth." If we were always passive in the hands of the Master He would show forth in and through us His marvellous grace and power.

The polishing of the shaft is always necessary. God uses all our experiences to equip us for life. Parental influence; the power of prayer as offered in our behalf by others; the education given us in the schools; the disappointments of life which seem almost to crush us; the sorrows which are indescribable; all these are like the touch of a master's hand, and forth from such a school and such a training we ought to come prepared to do the will of God.

The arrow was carried in the quiver and the quiver was near to the master's side. Nearness to God is essential if we are to be used of God. He chooses the vessel nearest His hand. This has always been true. The apostles, martyrs, missionaries, and saints who have finished their work and have gone on before, as well as those who live to-day, prove the statement that we must be in closest relationship with Christ if we are to be entrusted with the gift of power. It is when we are in the secret place of the Most High that we learn God's will concerning us. Many people do not know God's will because they live too much in the bustle and confusion of life. God speaks His best messages to us in whispers, not in thunder tones, and we must be still to know that He is God and study to be quiet that we may go forth from quietness to conquer. The practice of the quiet hour is the secret of many a soul's victorious service.

> Shut in with God alone,
> I spend the quiet hour;
> His mercy and His love I own,
> And seek His saving power
> Shut in with God alone;
> In meditation sweet,
> My spirit waits before the throne,
> Bowed low at Jesus' feet.
> Shut in with God alone;
> I praise His holy name,
> Who gave the Saviour to atone
> For all my sin and shame.
> Shut in with God alone;
> And yet I have no fear,

I rest beneath the cleansing blood,
And perfect love is here.

# CHAPTER IV
## *Starting Right*

"Every one over against his house," Nehemiah iii. 28. The first part of the Book of Nehemiah gives us a striking picture of destruction, and as we look about us we see a city in ruins: the walls are down; the homes have been destroyed; the people are in despair, so great is the desolation that even the temple has been defaced. When the tidings concerning the havoc which has been wrought in the city of Jerusalem reached Nehemiah he was well nigh heart-broken. Speaking about the story that had been brought to him he said, "And they said unto me, The remnant that are left of the captivity there in the province are in great affliction and reproach; the wall of Jerusalem also is broken down, and the gates thereof are burned with fire," Nehemiah i. 3. When he reaches the city of Jerusalem he goes about to view the ruins, and he thus describes his journey: "So I came to Jerusalem and was there three days. Then I told them of the hand of my God which was good upon me; as also the king's words that He had spoken unto me. And they said, Let us rise up and build. So they strengthened their hands for this good work," Nehemiah ii. 11 and 18.

This picture of despair as seen in the olden days in Jerusalem is almost if not altogether being repeated to-day. The case is really desperate. The need of Divine help in the re-construction of human lives has never been greater. Hosts of men find the following testimony a description of their own experience. It is a young university man who is speaking, and before a great crowd of people he says:--

"Probably nine out of every ten of you men standing in front of me know who I am and know my family well. You will no doubt be surprised to hear of the awful experiences through which I have gone during the past six months. Just six months ago, as most of you know, I was an active Christian worker, and there are many of you in front of me who as recently as last July sat and heard me preach. During the last six months trouble came upon me, and in a weak moment, losing faith in God, I took to drink, and sank as low as it is possible for any man to sink. Not even the prodigal in the parable could have fallen lower than I did. Disowned by my mother; cast aside by my brother and sisters; despised by the members and officers of the church to which I belonged and in which I preached, I was in every respect an outcast. Just before Christmas, whilst tramping on the road, I actually took the shirt off my back to sell it for drink, so miserable was I. My nights I spent in the open fields, waking in the morning covered with frost. Something seemed to compel me to attend the meetings in this city. I attended night after night, and although the singing and the address had a wonderful effect upon me, I kept struggling against the working of the Spirit, until the singing of the chorus "I am Included," brought home to me as never before, the fact that even I, wretched outcast that I was, had not gone too far. I then and there made up my mind to accept the promise of John iii. 16. From that time I have realized, as never before, that Christ went to Calvary not so much for the world, as He did for me. And I intend to devote the rest of my life to winning souls for Him."

There is surely cause for great alarm because of the present condition of affairs, and for the following reasons: Home life is not what it used to be. In the olden times the home was a harbour into which tempest-tossed souls came day after day, and thus protected, had time to regain lost strength and go forth again to battle with the storm. It was once true that fathers were priests in their own households and mothers were saints. The best memory that some of us have is that which centres in a home where love ruled and reigned; where Christ was honoured; where the Bible was read, explained and loved, and where the very atmosphere was like heaven. In many instances to-day this is missing and he is to be pitied who has not such a memory as this, and such an influence for good in his life. The family altar in too many households has been broken down or given up. "What led you to Christ?" was the question asked of a distinguished Christian worker. And the answer quickly given was, "My father's prayers at the family altar. They followed me through my manhood and compelled me eventually to accept Christ." When the family altar is gone from a home, it is like the taking away of a strong foundation from a building or depriving the arch of its keystone. Better sacrifice everything than this spirit and practice of prayer in the home.

It is barely possible that because of conditions family prayers may not be conducted to-day as in other days, but there is at least time for a verse of scripture and a prayer out of a full heart, and the influence of even so brief a service will keep the members of the household from many a failure.

Church attendance is not what it once was. The old-fashioned family pew is a thing of the past in too many cases. In other days the father, the mother, and the children attended divine worship in the house of God. They sang the hymns of the church together; they worshipped God with the same spirit of devotion; they listened to the minister's preaching and they came forth from such a service clothed with a power that made them able to stand against the mightiest influences for evil. Because the family pew is out of date many boys are wandering, and many girls have gone astray.

With the beginning of the fourth chapter of Nehemiah there is a change in the story as told by the Prophet. There is a ring of triumph when he announces: "So built we the wall; and all the wall was joined together unto the half thereof; for the people had a mind to work," Nehemiah iv. 6. And the completeness of his work is described when he says: "Now it came to pass when the wall was built, and I had set up the doors, and the porters and the singers and the Levites were appointed ..." Nehemiah vii. 1. I am sure it is quite true that out from all the despair which sometimes appals us, we shall come into the same complete victory. But if we are to win others to Christ and if our work is to be a work of prevention, so that our children shall not go astray and our friends may not wander, then it will be essential that we should, like Nehemiah of old, begin to build everyone over against his own house. It is a sad thing to find so many people in the world who are a public success and a private failure. Great superintendents of Sunday Schools, and poor fathers; experienced Sunday School teachers, and inconsistent in their own homes; eloquent preachers and poor illustrations of the spirit of Jesus; famed for piety as revealed to the public eye and quite as famed for lack of piety, when living out of the lime light, in the common round of daily duties with those who know us best and ought to speak of us most highly.

If our work is to be as God would have it where shall it begin? By all means let it begin with ourselves. There is a text of Scripture which every Christian must say over and over. He might begin the day with it and it might not be amiss for him to say it over before he closes his eyes in sleep. "Search me, O God, and know my heart; try me and know my thoughts; and see if there be any wicked way in me,"

Psalm cxxxix. 23, 24. It is quite unnecessary to study the methods of men if we cannot bear the test of God's searching eye.

We must be right in our own homes. In a meeting conducted recently in Wales a gentleman rose to say: "I came to the meeting on Friday afternoon and made a covenant with God that I would speak to someone about Christ. It laid so hold of my heart that I went home and spoke to my little girl. I asked her if she loved the Lord Jesus Christ, and she said, 'Yes, I do.' I said, 'Will you accept Jesus as your personal Saviour?' 'Yes, I am willing to' she said. I went to the steel works, and had been praying that God would use me. I asked the young man with whom I was working if he were a Christian. He looked black at me, but I asked him to be honest before God. In a moment his face changed as he said without hesitation, 'I will accept Jesus as my Saviour now.'

"I was working during the night, and it came to food time, so I asked several of the men if they would come into the smith shop and have a word of prayer. There was a young man there whose little boy I had spoken to. This young man came to me at three o'clock in the morning to tell me that he would accept Jesus as his personal Saviour. I asked some of the men if they would come up to my house and have a little prayer meeting after work, at six o'clock in the morning. They came up and I spoke to them, quoting the texts John iii. 16 and John v. 24. Some of the men present were not saved. I asked them if they really understood the Scriptures, and they told me they did. 'Now,' I said, 'will you not accept Jesus as your personal Saviour?' and one who was in the smith shop told me that he had definitely given himself to God at three o'clock that morning. Then I asked a boy of fifteen if he understood the words. 'Yes,' he said, so I asked him if he would not accept Christ. 'Yes' he replied, 'I will.' The following night I spoke to another in the works, concerning his soul, and asked him if he had fully surrendered, because I knew he was in trouble. About one o'clock I spoke to him and said, 'Will you give yourself to the Lord now?' 'No,' he said, 'not now.' 'Well,' I said, 'come to the smith shop at food time and have a word of prayer.' After food time he came out, and started again at his work. Presently he came across to me. 'Well,' I said, 'have you fully surrendered?' 'Yes, Tom,' he said, 'I have given myself to Christ, now.'"

Beginning in the home it is quite easy to go out into a wider circle and serve. The tendency, however, is to begin in some public place, and oftentimes because of this we fail to win those who work by our side, who sit with us at our own table and who live with us day after day and for whom we are specially responsible. It will also be necessary for us to enlarge the circle and reach the people in our own places of business. Two business men journeyed into a New England city together for twenty years. One of them was a Christian, the other was not. They were both dying the same day, and the man who was not a Christian when he heard that his friend was dying, had a right to say to his wife, as he did, "It is a strange thing that my friend and I have known each other so well, and love each other so dearly, that he has allowed me to come to this day without a warning."

A business man rose in a meeting to say, "I have been greatly concerned about one young man who works in my office. I asked him if he would not come to the office a little earlier this morning. When he came and we were alone I asked him if he knew why I had got him to come a little earlier. When he told me that he did not, I said to him 'I am a Christian, I have never spoken to you about Christ and I have asked you to come this morning that I might explain the way to you and urge you to take your stand for Him.' That morning I had the great joy of leading my employee to Christ. I gave him a little pocket Testament in which I wrote his name, and under his name I wrote this Scripture, 'Thou art my son, this day have I begotten thee,' and after that I signed my name. Three days later," said the business man, "the young man of whom I speak, led three others to Christ, one of them was the head book-keeper in my office."

If we are to be successful soul winners it is essential not only that we should get right with God but that we should keep right with Him. There must be a quick confession of sin and a quick turning away from all that would work against Christ. Our friends with whom we live and labour are keen critics, and as a rule, just ones. They know when we are wrong and nothing so hinders a testimony as to allow a wrong to go unrighted. When before our own households and with those who know us best, and by whose side we toil, in shop, or store, or office, or with those whom we employ, we keep ourselves unspotted from the world, we have an unanswerable argument for Christ and a testimony as regards the value of following Him which cannot be gainsayed.

# CHAPTER V
## *No Man cared for my Soul*

"No man cared for my soul," Psalm cxlii. 4. All about us people are saying
these words, and they really think we do not care. I believe there has never been a
story of a man in which was found more contrast than in this account of the man
who sobs out the words, "No man cared for my soul." He is a shepherd boy, then a
king, a saint, writing the twenty-third Psalm, then suddenly turned into a sinner
blackening the pages of the Old Testament with the story of his transgressions. The
world has not had better poetry than that which came from the heart and brain of
this marvellous man. In addition to all this, he is a musician, and all through the
Psalms he is keeping time to heaven's music until, when he comes to the close of
the Psalter, he stands like the leader of a mighty chorus, and calls upon every living breathing being to praise the Lord. He is a pursuer of men, and the hosts of the
enemy run and cry and flee before him.

Suddenly the scene is changed. He is himself pursued. He is in the cave of En-
gedi. The cave is dark, and it is in the gloom that we hear him crying out, "I looked
upon my right hand and beheld, but there was no man that would know me: refuge
failed me." And as he said this I think he must have said, with a sob, "No man cared
for my soul." But it is not my intention so much to tell the story of this man whose
life was so filled with contrasts, but rather to speak of those who live to-day, and
who think they have a right to use the same words as the Psalmist, "No man cared
for my soul."

They walk on the streets of our cities; they live in our homes; they meet us in
our places of business; they are members of our circle of friends; they know that we
are Christians, and they are often thinking or saying, "No man cared for my soul."
It is strange that we should permit this, because we read in the Bible, "He that
believeth not is condemned already." "He that hath not the Son of God hath not
life, but the wrath of God abideth on him." It seems strange that one could say he
believes the Bible to be true; that he accepts these statements concerning the one
who is not a Christian, and yet lives and works and associates with him and never

speaks to him about the salvation of his soul.

It would seem as if they at least had a right to say, "No man *seems* to care." But some may say, "They have the Church, and the doors are wide open; they have the minister, and his message is faithful." Yet, the average man who sits in church and listens to the most impassioned appeal of the preacher, rarely considers the sermon personal. He finds himself saying, sometimes against his will, that the preacher is professional, that his plea is perfunctory, and so he goes out of church and says again, "No man *seems* to care for my soul."

There came into my church in an Eastern city a man who worshipped with us for a time. His family were in the mountains. I made it a rule never to allow one to attend the church that I did not speak to him personally. One day I called on this business man. He took me into his private office. When I took him by the hand I said, "I have come to ask you to be a Christian." He looked at me in amazement; and I said, "I am not asking you to join my church, that may not be the church of your choice, but I am asking you to be a Christian." He drew his hand out of mine, walked away to the window, and stood looking down upon the busy street for fully five minutes. I thought I had offended him. Then he came back, and, brushing the tears out of his eyes, he took my hand again and said, "It is the first invitation to be a Christian I have ever had in all my life. Nobody ever asked me before. My mother never asked me; my wife has never asked me; no minister has ever asked me." Then, sinking back into the chair by his table, he used the words which are almost identical with the words of David, "I thought no one cared."

Such men are all around us; men in deepest need; men with sore aching hearts. There was a man in an American city who occupied a high position among men. He took his own life. Under the stress of political excitement he misappropriated the funds of the bank, thinking he could repay them, and in his beautiful home he put the revolver to his temple and shot himself. The saddest letter I have ever seen was written by that man. He wrote to his wife asking her forgiveness. He told her to pray for the children whom he had dishonoured. Then he concluded his farewell letter with this statement: "Through all the months I have been wishing somebody would speak to me about becoming a Christian." In the light of such facts I believe that what we need in these days is not so much, more men to preach--although that would be a great blessing--as people in the church who will be absolutely consistent. If they say they believe God's Word to be true, they must speak to those over whom they have an influence, about the personal acceptance of Christ.

I was waiting one day outside the office of the Governor of one the Western States, and while I waited, the Lieutenant-Governor spoke to me. He said, "I was in your service last night, and I want to take issue with you on what you said. You told your hearers to go up and down the streets asking the people to become Christians. I think if anyone should come into my office and ask me to become a Christian I should tell him to go about his business." "You surely misunderstood me," I said; "what I told them was this, that if a business man was not a Christian, his friend who is a Christian ought to speak to him kindly about his soul." I had been introduced to the Lieutenant-Governor by one of the great politicians of the State, who was a sincere Christian, and I said, "Suppose our mutual friend here should come to you and say, 'I am a Christian. I think it is the best thing for a man to be a Christian. I am not always what I would like to be myself, but I should like to invite you to become a Christian.' Then suppose he should tell you what a strength and help it had been to him, what would you say to him?" He looked at me for a moment, and said, "I think I should say 'Thank you.'" I am sure thousands could be won to Jesus Christ if the members of the Church were consistent in the matter of living in Christ and giving an invitation to people to become acquainted with Him.

It is not fair to charge the minister with being professional, nor to say that in his appeal he is perfunctory. Nor is it always just to criticize those who are in the church, for not speaking to the unsaved, for there may be an explanation. Sometimes we feel a sense of our own unworthiness. There are business men who know that if they should speak to their employees, the first speech would have to be a confession of failure. There are women who know that if they should go to their husbands or children, and ask them to come to Christ, they would have first of all to say, "You must forgive my inconsistency." There are fathers who know that they could not go to their homes and call their children around them, and bid them come to Christ without first saying, "You must forgive your father." But if a confession is necessary, then make it. It is sometimes a sense of unworthiness that seals one's lips, but remember if you have a friend who is not a Christian, and to whom you have never spoken of Christ, your friend counts you inconsistent because of your failure.

I said to the officers in my church one evening, "How many of you have ever led a soul to Christ?" About half of them said they never had. One officer said, "That is a sharp question for me. If you will excuse me I will go home and speak to my children, to-night." He did so, and I received two of his sons into the church shortly after.

Again, we seem to have failed to warn our friends because we have such a slight conception of the meaning of the word "Lost." A mother in Chicago one day carried her little baby over to the doctor, and said, "Doctor, look into this baby's eyes, something has gone wrong with them." The doctor took the little child and held it in his arms so that the light would strike its face, He gazed at it only for a moment, then, putting it back into its mother's arms, he shook his head, and the mother said quickly, "Doctor, what is it?" And he said, "Madam, your baby is going blind. There is no power in this world that can make him see." She held the baby in her arms close up against her heart. Then with a cry she fell to the floor in a swoon, saying as she fell, "My God--blind!" I think any parent must know how she felt. But Jesus said, "Better to be maimed, and halt, and blind than to be lost."

If you believe the Bible you cannot be indifferent. But you say, some would not like to have you speak to them. I have been twenty-seven years a minister, and have spoken to all classes and conditions of men and women, and only in one single instance have I ever been rebuked. I was once asked to speak to the president of a bank. I went into his office, and was introduced to him by the pastor with whom I was staying. I said, "My friend is very interested in you, and I wish I could lead you to Christ." He looked at me in perfect amazement. Then, rising from the chair, he took me by the hand, and said, "Thank you, sir." I saw him that night, make his way down the crowded aisle of the church, give the minister his hand, and say, "I will."

But I had a sad experience at college. I roomed with a man when I was a student for the ministry, and never spoke to him about his soul. When the day of my graduation came, and I was bidding him good-bye, he said, "By the way, why have you never spoken to me about becoming a Christian?" I would rather he had struck me. I said, "Because I thought you did not care." "Care!" he said. "There has never been a day that I did not want you to speak; there has never been a night that I did not hope you would speak." I lost an opportunity. I fear some day, I must answer for it.

You had an idea that you had no influence, but you must remember that when you speak in the name of Jesus Christ, God stands back of you; that when you plead for the salvation of a person, all the power of heaven is working through you. Some may ask, What is the best time to speak to my friends about Christ? I should say, speak to them when they are in trouble, seek them out when others are being saved, but, best of all, go to them when the Spirit of God says go, that is the best time. Whenever God says "Go," He is always making ready the heart for our coming. I was one day walking down the streets of an American city with a Methodist minister, when he said to me, "What would you do if you were impressed that you should speak to a man?" I said, "Speak to him." He said, "But this man has not been in church for thirteen years." "Nevertheless," I said, "speak to him." He turned and made his way to the great house where this business man lived. He rang the bell, and the door was opened by the gentleman himself, who said, "Doctor, I am glad to see you. I have been in all day thinking you might come." And in a very few minutes he was kneeling in the library with this gentleman whom he quickly led to Christ.

A year later I was passing through the city of Chicago, when, picking up a newspaper, I noticed that this man whom the minister had won to Christ, had died suddenly. I got a letter from the minister not long afterwards, and he said, "I was with him when he died. He sent a messenger for me to come and see him, and when I arrived he turned his face towards mine and said, "Dr ----, thank you for coming that day, for if you had missed that day, I might have missed this. Then he began to sing as best he could. He raised himself on his pillow, with his arms outreaching, and said, "Jesus Lover of My soul," and passed away. The minister's letter was marked with tears, and down at the foot of it was written this sentence; "God helping me, I will never hesitate again." They are all about us, men with aching hearts, men caught by the power of sin, young people and older people as well. They are waiting. Preaching may not win them; singing may not touch them. But personal effort will.

I might change the text and make it read: "The world does not care for your soul," You may win it, and it will mock you. Satan does not care for your soul. He will fascinate you and snare you, and when you say, "Oh, wretched man that I am! who shall deliver me from the body of this death?" there will be no deliverance. But

God cares. Christ cares. The minister cares, and thousands of others care. Some are saying, "What must I do to be a Christian?" A gentleman once said to me, "I do not love God." Another person once said, "You talk about love for Christ; is it like love for my mother, because if it is I have not got it." No, it is not like that. That is not the first step in the way. Tell them God does not say, "Love me, and I will save you." God says, "Trust me. Accept my conditions, believe on my Son and follow Him."

There was a great man in a Western city who had a little girl who was deaf and dumb. He loved his child so much that he would not allow anybody to teach her. She had a kind of sign language which they both understood, but nobody else was allowed to teach her. This gentleman at one time had occasion to leave home and go abroad. He could not take his daughter with him, so his minister persuaded him to send her over to an institution where she could be taught to use the sign language of the deaf and dumb. He took her over himself, never for a moment imagining that she would learn to speak with her lips, as she did. The months passed by, and when the father returned, the minister went with him to see his child in the institution. The little girl had been told that he was coming, and looking out of the window she saw her father coming through the gate. She sprang to the door, and ran down the steps, and along the walk until she reached her father. Then she climbed up into his arms, and, putting her lips up against his ear, she said, "Father, I love you, I love you." The great man held her out at arm's length, looked into her face, then pressed her more closely to his heart and fell in a faint--when he recovered consciousness he was sobbing. All the day he kept saying, "I have heard her speak, and she loves me, she loves me." So tell the people very plainly that God does not say, "Love me." He says, "Believe on me; trust me; follow me." Then ask them, Will you do it? And if they will follow Him, having accepted His Son as their Saviour, and with his help having turned from sin, then if they will obey Him, they will come to love Him with all their hearts.

# CHAPTER VI
## *Winning the Young*

"There is a lad here," John vi. 9. Jesus had just crossed over the sea of Galilee and, attracted by the miracles which he had wrought, great multitudes had followed after Him. In order that He might escape the throng, He went up into a mountain and there He sat with His disciples. When the Master saw the great company stretching out on every side of Him He said unto Philip, "Whence shall we buy bread that these may eat." Philip was so amazed at the crowd that he answered Him, "Two hundred pennyworth of bread is not sufficient for them, that every one of them may take a little." Then one of His disciples, Andrew, Simon Peter's brother, said unto Him, "*There is a lad here* which hath five barley loaves and two small fishes." Then Jesus made the multitude sit down, and took the loaves and gave to the disciples, and the disciples to them that were seated, and likewise of the fishes as much as they would, and when they were filled, the fragments that remained filled twelve baskets.

The presence of this lad and the service which he rendered to Jesus, as well as the use which the Master made of him, all help us to teach our lesson. Youth is the time to turn to Christ. The wise man knew this when he said, "Remember now thy Creator in the days of thy youth; while the evil days come not, nor the years draw nigh; when thou shalt say, I have no pleasure in them." Sin has not so strong a hold upon a life in the time of youth, therefore it is the easiest time to turn to Christ.

I once heard a man tell the story of his special work among outcast men and women, and when I asked him he told me how he himself was converted. He said that as a boy in London, he was left one day in charge of the private office. He said "I wanted to write a letter and I took the firm's note-paper; I used one of their envelopes, and when I wanted postage I opened the private drawer of the safe, the door of which was swinging open, and took out one postage stamp, and when I put this stamp upon my letter and dropped it into the post-box I felt as if I had dropped my character with it. That was the beginning, and the end was a prison cell, for I went from one form of thieving to another until I was obliged to pay the penalty. I found Christ while I was in prison, but I feel as if the mark of my early sin would never leave me. I would urge every boy to accept Christ," he said, "before the cords of sin bind him too securely."

When one reaches the age of eighteen he finds it extremely difficult to turn away from the sins that are mastering him, and when he passes beyond twenty years of age, the tide against him is extremely heavy. The critical time in the life of boys and girls is from twelve to twenty. If they do not accept Christ during these years, it is wellnigh impossible to win them. If this is true then we must make the most of the opportunities of influencing the youth whom God is ever bringing before us.

The Scripture used in connection with this feeding of the multitude is a good illustration. It is a lad who confronts us, and this is, as has been said, the favourable time for bringing Christian influence to bear upon him. There is a time in the life of every boy when it is comparatively easy to win him to Christ. Parents surely know this, and Sunday school teachers may easily discover it. "How did you come to Christ?" said a New York minister to a little boy. His reply was, "My Sunday school teacher took me last Sunday out into the park. She drew me away from the crowd and took her seat beside me. She asked me if I would become a Christian. I felt that I ought to do so, and because her invitation was so definite, and she seemed so interested, I told her I would do so, and because I am a Christian I went to join the Church."

Too much cannot be said in favour of reaching the young while they are in the days of their youth. Recently in an audience of 4500 people I found that at least 400 of the audience came to Christ under 10 years of age; between 10 and 12, 600; between 12 and 14, 600; between 14 and 16, about 1000; between 16 and 20, fully one half, and in the entire audience not more than 25 people came to Christ after they were 30 years of age. Five hundred ministers were in the same audience. The majority of them were converted before they were 16 years of age; 40 of them between 16 and 20; and only 15 out of the 500 ministers were converted after they were 20. This in itself is an unanswerable argument in favour of personal work for the young.

The lad is here now before us, but he will soon be gone. Boys quickly grow into manhood. As a rule religious influence weakens as they pass on, while the power of sin increases. Many young men would turn to Christ if they thought they could, but it seems to them that the attraction towards evil is almost, if not quite irresistible. I recently heard a Christian gentleman speaking before a great audience in London. He was telling of his going over the Alps in the care of a trusted guide. As they came to one of the most dangerous places in the journey his guide stopped him, and said, "Do you see those footprints off here to the right?" The gentleman said he did, plainly. "Do you notice," said the guide, "how they get farther and farther apart?" And when asked to give an explanation he said that a week before a young telegraph operator had attempted to cross the mountains without a guide, that just at the place where they were standing his hat blew off, and, without thinking, he reached out after it, lost his balance and started to fall. In trying to recover himself he started down the mountain to the right. The way was all covered with snow; when once he started he could not stop; farther and farther apart were his footprints until at last they were lost on the edge of a great abyss. He had gone over to his death. It is thus that young men go to destruction. Because they do, we ought to be instant in season and out of season in seeking to arrest their downward progress.

When Jesus took the loaves and fishes in the possession of the lad and brought to bear upon them his own marvellous power, the results were great. No one realises what is being accomplished when he assists or influences a boy. I am wondering what that minister, who led Spurgeon to Christ, thinks of his work now that he sees it from the heavenly standpoint, and I have many times thought I should like to ask the business man who spoke to D.L. Moody about his soul, what estimate he puts upon the importance of the work he did that day. To win a boy to Christ may be to turn towards the Master one who may one day move the world for Christ.

A great number of Chinese young men have come from their native land to study in the educational institutions of the United States. Some of them have found Christ in these institutions, others have passed through their course of study and returned to their native land without a hope in the Saviour. What a marvellous work might have been accomplished if the Christian students in these educational institutions had set themselves to win these Chinese boys. The students in China are to have an increasing influence in the Government, and if the majority of them had been led to Christ, the whole Chinese Government might have been powerfully affected. Some years ago there came to the United States a little Chinese boy. He was sent to a New England educational institution, and made his home in the house of a very humble woman. She knew Christ and loved Him, and she recognised the presence of this little boy as presenting an opportunity for service. She treated him as if he were her own child. She mothered him and grew to love him. She taught him how to read the Bible and she told him the story of Jesus and His love. That little boy came to Christ. He passed through the educational institution, went back to China to exercise his strongest influence for righteousness, and has recently been entrusted with the commission of bringing to the United States a number of other Chinese boys, all of whom, it is said, he will place in institutions that are Christian. The poor woman in New England did not realise that when she led one boy to Christ that she was touching forty others. This is the fascination of Christian work.

Some of the noblest men and women the Church has ever known came to Christ in youth. Polycarp, Matthew Henry, Jonathan Edwards, the immortal Watts, John Hall, and a countless host of others who have served conspicuously in the advancement of the Kingdom of God, came to Christ before they were fifteen years of age, some of them coming as early as seven. The lad is here, it will be a pity if we allow him to grow to manhood without a hope in Christ all because we do not seek to win him.

# CHAPTER VII
## *Winning and Holding*

"From a child thou hast known the Holy Scriptures, which are able to make thee wise unto salvation through faith which is in Christ Jesus," 2 Timothy iii. 15. Timothy's inheritance was invaluable. His equipment was superb, and his experience from the day of his birth until the end of his life upon earth, ideal. He had a good grandmother. Evidently she influenced him profoundly. I am quite sure that his parents too must have fulfilled their obligations to their child, and in addition to his own immediate ancestry, he had Paul, the Apostle, who looked upon him as a son in the Gospel, and honoured him by sending him his last message when he said, "I have fought a good fight, I have finished my course, I have kept the faith; henceforth there is laid up for me a crown of righteousness, which the Lord, the righteous Judge, shall give me at that day, and not to me only, but to all them also that love His appearing. Do thy diligence to come shortly unto me" 2 Timothy iv. 7-9.

It is a great loss to any child to be deprived of what Timothy had. We may not all be rich, and we certainly cannot all be great, but we may all be true and faithful as parents, and when a child has such an inheritance he is well started in life. It is because children do not have this that many of them drift. Given a good ancestry it is comparatively easy to draw children to Christ, and even to draw them back when once they have wandered. It is the testimony of rescue mission workers that when they have the privilege of appealing to lost and ruined men in the name of a mother who was saintly and a father who was true to Christ, they have a hold upon an almost irresistible force, to bring the wanderer back to the faith of his father and the teaching of his mother.

There is the sorest need to-day of a special and continued interest in behalf of our young people. David Starr Jordan is authority for the statement that "one-third of the young men of America are wasting themselves through intemperate habits and accompanying vices," the conditions in other lands are also very serious. The secretary of the College Association of North America has been quoted as saying that there are twelve thousand college men in New York City alone who are down and out through vice. "Talk of the ravages of war. The ravages of war, pestilence and disease combined are as nothing compared with the awful moral ravages wrought in the teen period. The shores are strewn thick with the wasted lives of those who have been wrecked in youth."

"We have been seeking results too far afield and overlooking great opportunities near at hand. If you take a census of a Christian congregation and ask those who were converted before their eighteenth birthday to rise, five-sixths of your congregation will stand. This means that five-sixths of all the people who give themselves to Christ do it on the under side of the eighteenth year. Put beside this the fact that we have more than 12,000,000 children and youth in the Protestant Sunday Schools of America under eighteen years of age and you will see that our great evangelistic opportunity does not lie outside of the Church, but inside, in the Sunday School department. Here we have a vast army, ready and waiting for the Christian call."[2]

It is one thing to lead souls to Christ, it is quite another thing to hold them when once they have been won. The serious time for drifting is between the ages of twelve and twenty. If we could but safeguard these years we would hold for the Church many who drift out upon the sea of life, make shipwreck of their hopes and break the hearts of those who are interested in them.

"An investigation in the Wesleyan Church of England showed that only ten

---

2   Rev Edgar Blake.

per cent of the Sunday School were held in active membership in the Church. Ten per cent. were held in a merely nominal relationship. Eighty per cent. were lost entirely. This is a fair statement of the situation in many churches. We have lost multitudes of our youth who might have been saved if they had been properly cared for.

"At the very time the Church loses its grip upon the boys and girls the public school loses its grip also. The exodus begins about the fifth grade, and at the eighth grade fifty per cent. of the scholars have departed. At the twelfth grade, near the middle teens, ninety per cent. of the scholars have gone out from the public schools. Thus these two most powerful forces in the creation of character, the Church and the School, lose their hold upon youth at the same time.

"The home also loses its hold at this period. Up to his middle teens your youth accepts everything on the authority of others, but midway of the critical teen period there comes an awakening. The consciousness of his own personality, his right to make decisions for himself comes to him for the first time. Sometimes spontaneously, sometimes gradually, but always he breaks with authority. He insists upon deciding matters for himself. Parents may counsel, but they cannot determine[3]."

"A gentleman came to a friend of mine at the close of an address which he had delivered and said to him, 'I was much interested in what you said about the boys we lose. I teach a class of the finished product.' 'Where do you teach?' said I. 'In the State prison' he said. A few years ago seventy-five per cent. of the inmates of the Minnesota State prison were boys who had once been in Sunday School and had been permitted to drift away. The later teen age, sixteen to twenty, is the criminal period. It is an appalling thing that 12,000 children were brought before the courts of New York in 1909, and in the same year more than 15,000 boys and girls suffered arrest in Chicago. Our criminal ranks are added to, at the rate of 300,000 a year, and in the vast majority of cases the criminal course is begun in the teen age. Is it necessary? Is this awful waste--this moral havoc--unavoidable? I believe not. Recently a young man in his teens was convicted of theft in the court of Milwaukee. When the judge asked him if he had anything to say before sentence was pronounced upon him, the young man arose, pale with excitement and said, 'Your honour, my father and mother died when I was three years old. I never had anyone who loved or cared

---

3   Rev Edgar Blake.

for me. I have been kicked about all my life. Judge, I never would have been a thief if I had had a chance.' This is the pitiful plea of thousands who have been wrecked around us. They were not shepherded and they went astray."

There is a way to hold the majority of those whom we may win to the Saviour. A friend of mine led to Christ a young man who had gone to the very depths of sin and shame. He was a drunkard; he had disgraced his father's name; had broken his wife's heart, and when his little boy died he did not have enough money to bury the child decently; when the mother put the child in the grave the father was wild with drink, and he was buried without his father being present. But my friend won this man to Christ. After he was saved, every day for three weeks he went to sit by his side and talk with him; he guarded him at the critical time; he kept him from growing discouraged; he hindered him from drinking. To-day this man is himself one of the most noted rescue mission workers in the world, and is being used of God to save multitudes of men who like himself had gone down through drink.

It is what we are ourselves that largely counts in the holding of our friends for Christ. Paul wrote to Titus saying, "In all things showing thyself a pattern of good works ... that he that is of the contrary part may be ashamed, having no evil thing to say of you," which is only another way of saying that a Christian life is an unanswerable argument in favour of Christ. When our lives are right with God; when we keep ourselves unspotted from the world; when we quickly confess our own failure or wrongdoing; when we have a concern not only that others should be saved, but that they might do something for Christ after their salvation, it is comparatively easy to hold them, and to keep from drifting those who have just started along the way.

When my friend S.H. Hadley, the great rescue missionary, was lying in his coffin, a timid knock was heard at the door of the room where the body was resting. When the one who had knocked entered the room it was found that he was a drunkard, he had fallen from a high position to the very depths of despair, and as he stood timidly in the presence of the sorrowing friends of the great man, he said, "I thought I would like to come and look into his face and if I might be permitted to do so I would like to touch his hand. He did his best to win me while he was living and now that he is dead I cannot let his body be placed in the grave without coming here by the side of his casket to yield myself to Christ. All that he has said has followed me and I cannot get away from it."

Timothy knew the Scriptures, and a familiarity with God's Word is one of the best preventives in the case of drifting. One verse of Scripture committed to memory each day would help us to overcome the tempter; would keep us in loving touch with Jesus Christ; would inspire us to higher and holier living; and these suggestions made to those whom we win to Christ would keep them from wandering. It is the man who does not know his Bible who finds himself an easy prey to the wicked one. The ability to pray is also a God-given force which keeps us from drifting. When we read the Bible God talks to us; when we pray we talk to Him. We cannot always speak plainly of our condition to those about us, but we may tell Him what we are and what we wish we might have been. And while it is true that He knows before we speak, it is also true that in the telling we draw nearer to Him, and drawing nearer we absorb a little bit more of His spirit, and in that spirit we stand.

Service is also one of the surest preventives from wandering. It is when the brain is idle that evil thoughts master it; when the heart is given up to impure imaginations that we find it easy to fall. And it is when we are busy lifting others' burdens; making the way easier for others to travel; comforting those who are in distress; speaking a word of cheer to the cheerless, and above all, when we are seeking to lead others to Christ, that we ourselves grow in grace and in the knowledge of our Lord and Saviour Jesus Christ. If these things are true, and we know they are, then it is the duty of every Christian not only to seek to win another to Christ, but by all means to seek to hold him when once he is won, and that which we know holds us will keep others from stumbling.

The suggestions made above are for the young as well as the more mature. Young people will be interested in spiritual things if we have sufficient interest in them ourselves to make them attractive.

If we would show as great interest in helping to keep those whom we may have won for Christ, as we revealed when we were seeking them, fewer of them would drift.

# CHAPTER VIII
## *A Practical Illustration*

It will be a great day when the Church is aroused to the responsibility and privilege of personal work.

In Swansea, Wales, with Mr Charles M. Alexander, I had the satisfaction of conducting a mission in which I preached for an entire week on Soul Winning. I then urged the people to go forth and labour, and asked them to come back with their reports. These reports were thrilling. Often ten or twelve people would be standing at the one time waiting to speak. The following are only a few testimonies taken from the many:--

A minister said: "I spoke to a bright young fellow, under the influence of drink, as I was going home in the car last night. He got off the car when I did, so I stood at the street corner and talked with him for a few minutes. He told me that he had been a follower of the Lord Jesus many years ago, but had fallen away through bad company. I asked him to pray for himself. He said he could not, but asked me to pray for him. And there on that street corner I put my arm around his shoulder and we prayed together, and he has promised to come to the meeting to-night."

"About three years ago," said another, "I came in touch with a man who has been the biggest and most hardened scoffer I have had to contend with. He had such a sarcastic way of ridiculing the Lord Jesus Christ. But this last fortnight I have seen a distinct change in that young man's life. Last week, as we were working near to one another, I spoke to him and his eyes filled with tears. He said, 'I have decided to come out and accept Christ.' I could hardly credit it, but it has proved to be real, and when I see God moving in such a hard case as this, I have hope for every sinner in this city."

Another said, "I came to the Lord three years ago, one of the worst drunkards in Swansea. Since the Saviour found me, I have spoken to men on their death-beds. I have spoken to drunkards all over Swansea, but I neglected my own charge that God had given to me. Dr Chapman woke me up to approach my own household and children. It was the greatest struggle in all my life. I went to my two boys and put my hands on their shoulders saying, 'I want you to do something for Jesus and for your father.' They said, 'Father, we will do it.' Two of my boys came to the Albert Hall yesterday and gave their hearts to Jesus. This has been one of the most blessed weeks I have had since I was saved three years ago."

"On Thursday night I had been asking the Lord to lead me to the right one to speak to. He led me to a young man of sixteen years of age who was under tremendous conviction. He said, 'I think I will make a clean breast of it. I have done something,' and he told me his story. This young lad, in his employer's service for four years, last week, for the first time, began to steal. He turned out his pocket and showed me what he had. He said, 'What shall I do? I go to bed at night and I cannot sleep, it is haunting me.' I said, 'Look here, laddie, do this. Go to your master to-morrow morning, and make a clean breast of it and get the victory.' 'What about my situation?' said the boy. 'I will pray for you,' I said. 'If your master is so unkind as to dismiss you, come to me and I will see what I can do.' It was a long time before he gave in, but eventually he said, 'I will.' I prayed for him, and last night I got this letter: 'Victorious! Devil conquered; overjoyed. I cannot very well explain what I experienced so will be pleased to meet you on Thursday next in the mission at Albert Hall.'"

A week later this gentleman said: "I have a lot to thank God for these last ten days. I have had a glorious blessing. I can say with all humility, I have been on fire for Jesus. I had a letter yesterday from the young man whom I was talking about last Sunday. He says, 'Dear Friend, My only regret now is that I did not accept Jesus as my Saviour years ago. It would have saved me so much trouble. I explained everything to my master and handed him the article back. Then he gave me two-thirds of this particular article and burned the letter. So that is what I got for owning up.'"

Another said: "I do thank and praise God this morning for the great things He has done in my home. He has brought my children to trust in the Saviour. I have great pleasure in reporting that a brother at the works, to whom I spoke a week ago, has decided for Christ. One of the workers presented me with a Testament to give to that brother, who was in very poor circumstances, and he received it with joy. The following day he came to tell me that he had read a chapter to his wife. His wife is travelling the wrong way. They have five little children, and on Thursday I took them to the meeting. On Friday morning he came to thank me for taking them there, and told me that during his absence from the house, his eldest boy, of about ten years of age, had got into a Bible Reading Circle, led by a Christian boy, and he asked his father if he could spare sixpence for him to buy a Testament. What joy filled my heart and soul from the fact that I could present that little lad with a Testament, and I sent my own lad back a mile, yesterday, with it.

"I spoke to a dear Christian brother last night at the works. I asked him if his household were saved. 'I have one boy of sixteen not saved,' he said 'Brother, will you promise me to speak to him when you go home?' He went home and put his hand on the shoulder of the lad and gave him the invitation. The boy gladly promised to accept Jesus."

Continuing with the reports, one said: "Last night, in one of our public houses I spoke to a woman about Jesus. Years ago she had lost her husband and instead of going to God for comfort she had turned to drink. She became a drunkard and had separated from her children. When I spoke to her she said, 'I know I am a sinner. I am the worst woman in Swansea, but I want to be good.' 'Will you decide now?' we asked her. 'Yes,' she said. She came out into the cold biting wind and knelt in the open air, and there she sent up this simple prayer: 'Oh, God, although I am a bad woman, please make me good, for Jesus' sake.' Later she arose in a crowded meeting and told her story, concluding with this remark, 'By God's help I am going to be a child of God.'"

Another said: "On the second night of the mission I was led to speak to a dear brother who was a back-slider. I plead with him that evening to turn to Christ, but he did not come to a decision. The next night I went in and talked with him. I asked him again at the close of the meeting would he come back to the Lord Jesus Christ. He told me he could not come back that night. On the following night I went up and spoke to him again. When we got outside the building I said, 'I may not ever have the privilege of speaking to you again. Will you kindly give me your name? I will give you a guarantee that no one but God shall know about it. I want your name that I may pray for you.' On Tuesday night in the minor hall at the after meeting I searched for him. I had been praying continually every night and morning, and sometimes during the day. When I found him that night I said, 'You have withstood the Spirit of God long enough. Make a definite decision to-night to return to the Lord. If you do not care about coming to the front, fill out this card, but make up your mind to give yourself to Christ.' He took the card and filled it out. Then I said, 'You know the way of salvation because you have been that way before. When you get home tonight, will you kindly make a definite decision at your bedside?' And he told me he would."

Another gentleman rose to give his testimony and said: "I belong, as you know, to another city, but I want to speak a word to the glory of God, and for the encouragement of those who have taken up personal work for Him. Some two years ago in our city I spoke to one who was an inspector in the Police Force, but who is to-day the Chief Inspector of our Police, about the claims of Christ. He told me that I was the first one who had ever spoken to him as to how he stood in relation to these matters for a period of fifteen years. Having once broken the ice and spoken to him, I never gave him up.

"About two months ago I had occasion to go to the Police Court to ask his assistance on behalf of a woman who wanted an ejectment notice against another woman who was living in the same house. When he heard the name of the woman who wished to obtain the notice he refused to have anything to do with the matter. She had been a bad character. He said, 'I tell you candidly, she ought to be drowned for her cruelty to her children.' I said, 'You knew her once, but you do not know her now. How long is it since you saw her?' 'About nine weeks' he replied. 'Well,' I said, 'nine weeks ago she and her husband both came to Christ in our mission hall. For the first time in thirteen years they entered a place of worship. She had a black eye that covered over half her face, but both her husband and she are now Christians, and are faithfully following Christ to-day. And yet you call her a lost soul.' He said, 'Certainly I do. If there is a lost soul she is one.' 'Then Sir,' I said, striking him on the shoulder, 'Jesus came to seek and to save that which was lost. Jesus has saved that woman. When she comes on Monday night, Inspector, just look at her and see what Christ has wrought. I ask you to grant her request.' He shook himself free. 'Wait a moment, Inspector,' I said, 'I have never given up praying for you. You have risen to the position of Chief Inspector, but I want you not to forget Christ.'

"On the Thursday of the following week he came to my home. When I saw him there I was glad, for he had kept away from me for a long time. I said, 'I am glad to see you in my home.' He said, 'You will be more glad when you know why I have come. In my room the other night I knelt down and gave myself to Jesus Christ, and asked the Lord to save me.' I would ask those of you who are working for souls not to get disheartened and discouraged. When the mission ceases do not give up taking a personal interest in those for whom you are concerned.

"Some months ago I was sitting in the Assize Court in your city. I sat next to our Chief Inspector. The case that was being tried was one of attempted murder. As I sat there following the case this Chief Inspector turned to me and said, 'Why didn't they know Him on the road to Emmaus?' I said, 'I suppose because their eyes were holden.' He said, 'How did they know Him when they got to the home?' I said, 'Probably in the breaking of the bread.' 'Don't you think,' said he, 'that in the breaking of the bread they saw for the first time the marks of the wounds in His hands and knew Him by them?' What a difference Christ had made in the life of that Chief Inspector."

A man employed in the steel works rose in one of our meetings to say: "I made my covenant with God last Saturday. The burden was laid heavy on my heart on behalf of two souls. One of them was my own little girl. I spoke to her about Jesus, and she told me she would accept Him as her Saviour. I have been working this week on a shift that ran from ten o'clock at night to six o'clock in the morning. On Tuesday night I asked the Lord to pour out His blessing on our workmen. About one o'clock in the morning I had an opportunity of speaking to a young man. I asked him if he had accepted Jesus as his Saviour, and he said he had not. Then I asked him to be honest before God, and I said, 'Will you accept Him now?' With a smile he looked up at me and said, 'Tom, I will accept Jesus as my Saviour now.' I have brought some of my mates with me here to-day and I thank God for what He has done.

"Down at the works the other day there was a young man who came on duty at three o'clock in the morning. I knew he was troubled about his soul, and I spoke to him. I said, 'Are you in trouble about your soul?' He said, 'Yes, I am.' 'Well,' I said, 'Jesus has died to save you. Will you accept Him now?' He said to me, 'But, Tom, I have done this and that,' 'Well,' I said, 'Jesus has died for you, will you accept Him?' As he looked me straight in the face he said, 'Yes, I will.'

"I asked these men who had accepted Jesus and one or two others, to come up to my home at six o'clock when we finished work. As we went through the yard there was a boy about fifteen years of age standing there and we got him to come along with us. In my home we had a small meeting. I asked God to pour down

His blessing upon us. I asked one friend who was drifting, if he had ever accepted Christ, and he said at one time during a revival. I said, 'Praise God for that. He is willing to receive you back. Will you come?' and he said, 'At three o'clock this very morning, I came back to the Lord Jesus.' And then I turned to the boy of fifteen and said, 'Are you willing to accept the Saviour?' And he said he didn't think he was ready. I said, 'Well, my boy, if you don't, what will become of you?' He said, 'I will go to hell, I suppose.' Not long afterwards he accepted the Saviour.[4]

"Yesterday I could not sleep. I went home from my work. I was up in the morning with a burden on my heart because of the poor souls who were going to eternity without a Saviour. A young woman came to our house and started to sing 'Lord save Swansea,' and the words kept ringing in my ears. I went back to bed but could not sleep. I had no peace. I said, 'Well, Lord, I believe Thou hast surely started the work.' I went to the works last night. I did not feel very well as I had been up all day. I asked some of the men if they would come to a prayer meeting for the mission. We did not have much time before work commenced, but we went in and I asked one of the young fellows if he would accept Jesus. He replied, 'I must have time to think of it.' The next night I said to him, 'Johnnie, have you thought of what we spoke on last night?' and he said, 'I have been in trouble about my soul.' Before we had tea I asked him if he would accept Christ now. He said, 'I cannot do it now.' I said, 'God will give you strength.' We went into a little shop and I prayed for him. At three o'clock this morning I spoke to him again. 'Johnnie,' I said, 'can you see the way clear?' 'Yes,' he said, 'I can see the way clear now. I will accept Jesus as my personal Saviour.'"

# CHAPTER IX
## *Whosoever Will*

All classes of persons may do personal work if they will. A prominent business man in a Welsh city began to do this work and one morning spoke to eighteen people before breakfast. Several, to whom he spoke, accepted Christ. Making a further report of his work, he said. "An old man, about seventy years of age, whose face was

---

4   This man worked at night and slept during the day.

white and who appeared to be very ill, was leaning against the wall of a building near where I have my office. I said to him, 'Have you been to the mission?' 'No,' he said, 'I have not.' I then asked him if he had accepted Christ. 'Well,' he said, 'I have been a believer all my life.' I said, 'Are you saved?' 'I cannot say that,' he replied. 'Why?' I asked; 'God says, "He that believeth on the Son hath everlasting life. Do you believe that?' He stood staring me in the face for a few minutes, when he said, 'I never saw it in that light before.' I said, 'Will you take him at His word now?' And he replied, 'Yes, I will.'

"An old woman, an office cleaner, was making her way up the steps of a building. As I came up I recognised her, and said, 'Mrs Bell, I have been constrained to ask you if you have accepted Jesus Christ as your personal Saviour.' She looked at me, then setting down her broom she said, 'I want to, but no one has ever asked me,' 'Well,' I said, 'I ask you now. Will you accept Him just here? Will you say, Lord Jesus I accept Thee as my personal Saviour?' But she could not see the way. After some conversation I asked her if she would come to the hall and hear Dr Chapman and Mr Alexander, and she said she would go that evening. I was unable to go to the service myself that night and did not see her until the following Saturday morning. She came to my office and said, 'Since you spoke to me a few days ago I have had no peace. I am in an awful state, and unless I take Jesus I shall die. I am sure I shall because I cannot live like this.' And right there in the office she knelt down and accepted Christ as her Saviour and had the joy that always comes with this acceptance.

"This morning, the very first man I met, I was constrained to speak to about Jesus. I introduced myself by asking him if he had been to the mission. He said, 'Yes, I was at the Grand Theatre last Sunday afternoon.' 'Well,' I said, 'did you give your heart to the Lord?' 'No,' he replied, 'I did not.' I said 'Why?' 'Because I missed my opportunity,' was his answer. I said to Him, 'Will you do it now?' 'Do it now!' he exclaimed. 'Listen,' I said, 'God says in His Word. As many as received Him to them gave He power to become the sons of God. Will you receive Him? It is either one thing or the other--receive or reject. Your sins have been atoned for by His precious blood. Will you take Jesus now?' And suddenly, taking me by the hand, he said, 'I will.'

"From time to time I have been speaking to a young man belonging to a respectable family. At one time he was being brought up for the ministry, but he got into sin and sank very low. I persuaded him to attend one of the mission meetings. When Dr Chapman requested all those who wished prayer offered for themselves or for their loved ones, this poor fellow got up in the balcony and said, 'Pray for me.' Prayer was offered for him, and there, that night, he experienced the joy of salvation. He came to me the other day and said that he had definitely taken Jesus Christ as his Saviour."

One would not expect a police officer to be a personal worker, but many of them are, and notably so in Great Britain. Ex-Sergeant Wheeler of Oldham came to attend one of our meetings, and being asked to speak, he said: "Though an Ex-Sergeant, I am not an Ex-Christian. There are a large number of people who look upon a policeman from many standpoints, but it is very seldom that they see him in the position in which I am placed to-night. They have an idea that a policeman does not exist to preach the Gospel or to tell them about Jesus Christ, and it is Christian people who get that idea sometimes."

"I know a police sergeant in London who is a particular friend of mine and a great Christian worker. A lady went to one of our Provincial Police Conferences in connection with the Police Association and saw this big man who was so enthusiastic in connection with the work that the lady doubted his genuineness, and to satisfy her curiosity she ascertained his private address, travelled by rail from London, visited his home during his absence, and asked his wife what sort of a man he was. That is the way to find a man out. But she found that he was even a better man in the home than he was out of it. If you want to find what a man's character is, you do not ask about it on special occasions when he is on his guard, you ask what it is when he is at home, it is there that he unconsciously reveals it, and this revelation just because of its unconsciousness, proves invariably correct.

"When the Lord Jesus brought me out of darkness into the light, when He broke the fetters and snapped the chains eleven years ago, I went home and said to my wife, 'I am going to live for Jesus, and we will start here, at home. We will have family prayers--we were not a large family, only nine of us, and for the first time in their lives, my children heard their father pray; and there on my knees in all humility I pledged myself before God that I would do anything, make any sacrifice, if by so doing I could help a weaker brother and lift him out of the gutter. That is the way

I started. I am not what I ought to be, I am not what I hope to be, but, thank God, by His grace and love, I am what I am and not what I once was. The Lord changed my desires when he put a new heart within me. When I see a drunken man in the streets I do not pass him like I used to. My heart goes out to him and I look beyond the man in the streets to the life in the home he comes from, and see the misery there; but I thank God that He put the desire in my heart to try to help that brother. And how often opportunities present themselves.

"On one occasion at five o'clock on a Sunday morning in the month of August, a policeman and I were going along the street. There was a man standing at a gate near the corner. As we approached he said to me, 'Sergeant, can you get me a drink of whisky?' I said, 'That is rather a strange thing to ask a Sergeant of Police,' 'Well,' he said, 'I have plenty of bottled ale in my home, but it sticks in my throat.' I said, 'Do you take whisky when you are thirsty?' 'Yes,' he replied. I got into conversation with him and after a while I said to him, 'Do you ever go to a place of worship?' 'No,' he said, 'I don't, I pay a sovereign for a sitting.' 'That won't get you to heaven,' I said, and after a little further talk with him he remarked, 'Sergeant, I am all right financially, but wrong here, in my heart.' And then he said, 'Will you come to my home and pray for me?' 'Yes,' I replied, und we went. It was not far away, a fine home, a palace to mine, I thought, as I walked across the velvet carpet into the drawing-room. He brought a Bible and said, 'Read me something out of that.' And he sat down like a little child, to listen. I turned to Isaiah liii. 6, and read, 'All we like sheep have gone astray; we have turned everyone to his own way; and the Lord hath laid on Him the iniquity of us all.' 'Now,' I said, 'it starts with All and finishes with All, so we are both included.' Then I took him to John iii. 16, and then to the last chapter in the Book of Revelation, verse 17: 'And the Spirit and the Bride say, Come. And let him that heareth say, Come. And let him that is athirst--I stopped at that--and whosoever ...' 'Now,' I said, 'we will read it again. And after we had read it again we knelt down, and there in that large home I poured out my soul to God over that man. I plead for him, and while I prayed he said, 'Lord, if I am not too bad, save me.' I said, 'Amen.' And the Lord heard his prayer, and before I left the house he was a changed man. When I was leaving he came to the door and said, 'I never bargained for this, this morning, Sergeant.' The man who wanted whisky got Christ. He drank of something different, he drank of the living water which Christ spoke about at the well of Samaria when He said, 'Whosoever drinketh of the water that I shall give him shall never thirst; but the water that I shall give him shall be in him a well of water springing up into everlasting life.'"

"I left him and went back the following day. I rang the bell and he answered the door himself. I asked him how he was, and he said, 'Grand, I have had no whisky.' I went back a month later and he told me he was never so happy in all his life. He said, 'Do you remember me telling you I paid a sovereign for my sitting in church? Well, I occupy that pew myself now.' And that day he gave me a donation for the Christian Police Association and told me to call again at any time. That is what the Lord does when he changes a man's heart. There are many men to-day who may be all right financially; they may have a seat in God's House; they may be members of a Church and yet not be right at heart. I urge upon you, get right with God and you will have, not the peace of this world, but the peace that passeth all understanding.

"Something like seven years ago I went to some services in Manchester that were being conducted by Dr Torrey and Mr Alexander. At the close of these services I went to the front and took some Gospel literature that was there for distribution. When I got home and commenced my duties I began to give this literature to the policemen. I thought the policemen stood as much in need of it as anybody else. If he is a peacemaker, sometimes he is a peacebreaker, and with all due respect to him he is not always a law-abiding man.

"There were two booklets in which I was specially interested. One which was called 'God's Sure Promise,' asked several questions at the close, and then requested the reader to sign his name. The other was, 'Get Right with God.' I gave the latter to policemen on their beats, and asked them to read them carefully. I went on with my praying. One man received the book with great scorn. About a week after I visited this particular man, and with a smile upon his face he said, 'You remember those two booklets you gave me?' 'Yes,' I said. 'Well,' he said, 'the one called "God's Sure Promise" I tore up and put into the fire, the other I tore up and threw over the wall, but not before I read them both. Now, I have never got away from that, and about half an hour ago I came to the climax. I got down on my knees in the street, and now I can honestly say that God for Christ's sake has pardoned all my sins.' I felt overjoyed with his testimony, for he was the most scornful and bitter man in the division. I was so overjoyed that I walked round his beat with him, talking with him, and giving him words of encouragement. I can never forget that night. From ten o'clock until six in the morning it was one continual downpour of rain. We were soaked through. As we walked round I said, 'We will have a word of prayer.' We took off our helmets, knelt down on the pavement and there we had a little prayer meeting just about two o'clock in the morning. The showers of rain were nothing compared to the showers of blessing we had. I was so delighted when we went off duty that morning that I could not sleep.

"I came to Manchester when Dr Torrey was holding a meeting, and during the meeting I sent a note up to Dr Torrey saying that a policeman wanted to say something. However, the opportunity did not present itself that night. A week after that another policeman came to me and said, 'Sergeant, do you remember that booklet you gave me, "God's Sure Promise?"' I said, 'Yes.' 'Well,' he said, 'here it is signed.' Seven years have passed away since that time, and those two policeman and I have stood together on the platform many and many a time telling the story of Jesus and His love. We have had some meetings together and I have seen them speaking to hundreds of men and the Lord has blessed them both. If the Lord Jesus Christ can save a policeman, He can save anybody.

"I found that we existed for something more than locking up people. I wanted to arrest people in their sin, and going along the street one night in company with another constable we were called into a little house. The kind people there had taken in a woman off the street. She was lying on the floor in a very drunken condition, unconscious of everything around her. I knew this woman, she was about twenty-seven years of age. I made her acquaintance when I used to be on night duty. Every Saturday night or in the early hours of Sunday morning I used to find her door open--her home was in a little side street, that kind of people generally live in a side street. It was about three o'clock on Sunday morning when I walked in and saw the man lying on the floor and the wife who was also drunk, lying on a sofa. The next time I was on night duty I found the same door open, and this time the wife was lying on the floor and the man on the sofa, and both were drunk.

"These kind people that I spoke of, consented to keep the woman there while I went to see the husband. I got to the house but found that he had removed to a little room in a little back street. There he was lying on a bit of a shake-down. I roused him up and told him where he would find his wife. He said, 'What time is it?' I said, 'Three o'clock in the afternoon.' He had one shilling left and he took a cab and went and brought his wife home.

"A few days afterwards I got them both to sign the pledge. The man was about the same age as his wife. He told me he did not know the taste of tea and coffee, he drank nothing but beer. He only had the clothes he stood up in. Four months passed after he signed the pledge. I met him one night and he had on a black suit of clothes and a watch and guard in his pocket. I was delighted to see him. Some time after that I went to address a very large temperance meeting. The hall was packed, and when I went on to the platform who should be there but this young fellow occupying the chair. What a sight it was to me! He pointed out to me his wife in the audience. There she sat, all smiling and well dressed. Time went on and I was the means not only of keeping them to the pledge but of bringing them to Christ; the Christ of the Gospel; the Christ that has bridged the gulf between God and the gutter; between the saint and the sot; between the pew and the slum.

"Oh, what a pleasure it has been to see how that man works for Jesus. I went to his house some time after that. It was not in the back streets, although he worked there and got some people to sign the pledge. But he came out into the front street, and there was a knocker on his door. When I knocked, his wife admitted me into the sitting room. She told me that Sunday morning that her husband was out visiting the sick. I know that he brought many men to the Sunday morning Bible Class. He told me this story. 'Do you know,' he said, 'When I used to spend all my money in the public house, oftentimes on the holidays I would take the landlord's luggage to the station for the price of a pint of beer. Not long ago we had our holiday, and instead of taking the landlord's luggage to the station I had a man to carry mine, and as we were going up the street with this man walking in front of us we passed one of the public houses where I had often spent my wages. The landlord was standing at the door. When he saw me passing he said, 'What does this mean?' I said, 'It means that I am going to Ireland instead of thee.' That man is being used to-day in God's service. The blood of Jesus Christ cannot only save but it can keep."

# CHAPTER X
### *Conversion Is a Miracle*

When one turns from sin to Christ and thus becomes a new creature, it is entirely the work of God. He must feel a sense of his need and appreciate the power of the Saviour, but it is the power of the Holy Spirit of God that transforms him. The stories of men and women who have been brought to Christ are always thrilling.

Every Christian ought to be a soul winner, and however many other obligations may rest upon him, the obligation of introducing others to Jesus Christ is of the first importance. If our lives are right; if we are wholly submitted to Him; if we are quick to do His bidding; if we have a familiarity with the Scriptures; if we have a confidence in the willingness of God to save; then we are emboldened to seek the lost and turn to those who are furthest away from Christ.

To know that others have been won to Him is always an inspiration. Recently in one of our meetings in New York, the Salvation Army forces came to assist us, and they brought with them some men and women whose stories of conversion were truly remarkable. In quick succession they appeared before an audience of several thousand.

The first speaker modestly began by saying: "What I am this afternoon, I am by the grace of God. For years and years I had been nothing but an every-day drunkard. Not far from where the Salvation Army held their open air meetings was an old lamp post. One Sunday afternoon I heard their music and their singing, and I made my way to this lamp post. If it had not been there I believe I would never have been saved, for I was so intoxicated I could not stand.

"After the meeting was over one of the sisters came to me and said, 'My brother, wont you come along to the meeting? You need salvation.' 'Yes,' I said, 'I need something better than what I have got.' At the same time I did not go--I finished up the day in the saloon. I came out into the open air again and the devil said, 'You cannot mix with these people they are too far above you.' By and by there came a man who said he had been every bit as bad as I was, and he told me how his life had been changed. And my eyes were opened then and there, and I kept going to the meetings and I got some decent clothes, and a home of my own--though I had been working every day I had not a home to go to--but when I was converted all became changed. And now I am perfectly happy. My life is completely made over. I never think of drink and have no desire for it. I have a happy home and a "little lump of glory" for a wife.

"When I first became a Christian the devil said to me, 'You cannot stay there with those people, there is a whisky bill you have not yet paid. Suppose you are out in one of those open air meetings and the saloon keeper should see you and say, 'Why, he owes me six dollars,' what could you say then?' I went to that saloon keeper and said to him, 'How much do I owe you?' And he said, 'Six dollars.' 'Well,' I said, 'I want to pay it.' I did pay it then and there, and glory to God He has kept me from then to this day."

The next testimony was that of a former anarchist. Before he was converted he did not have a shirt to his back. He is now a business man in New York City, and prosperous.

"It was about eighteen years ago that I was with a group of men in a back street attending a meeting of anarchists, when the police came along and broke up the meeting. I made off as fast as I could, but I did not get away fast enough, for the police officer caught me by the arm and took me away to prison. While I was there the Salvation Army came to preach to us. Thank God for that night! It was the first time I had heard salvation preached, for I come from the stock of Abraham, Isaac, and Jacob. When I got out of goal I went to the Salvation Army. There stood on the platform that night two girls. They told me about Jesus. They spoke of salvation for the drunkard, but that did not appeal to me; they spoke of salvation for the unbeliever, but that did not appeal to me; and when they spoke of salvation for the thief, neither did that appeal to me. Then one night they said salvation is for the Jew. I said to myself, 'That means me.' I came forward that night and got rid of my wretchedness and my misery; I came for salvation, and the Jew got salvation.'

"I moved away from the Bowery, for that was where I spent most of my time. I have walked down the Bowery many a night with not a place to lie down in, with not fifteen cents to pay for a bed, and not a shirt to my back. Thank God, I moved away from the Bowery. I started in business myself. To-day I have a splendid business connected with twenty houses on Broadway. Hallelujah! Godlessness, sin, vice, takes a man off Broadway and puts him on the Bowery; salvation takes a man from the Bowery and puts him on Broadway."

In the year 1880, the second convert in the Salvation Army in the United States was made, and after years of testing he came before us to speak as follows: "I started to drink when about thirteen years of age, and I kept drinking till the Salvation Army came to New York in 1880. I read in the papers about seven sisters coming over to open up the forces in the United States. There used to be an old lady who came to our house to see my mother. She was a Methodist, and my mother was also a Methodist. She used to come there like an old grandmother and darn stockings. One day she said she would like to go to the Salvation Army, and asked me to take her. I was leading such a dissipated and drunken life, that I had no money to pay the car fare, but she slipped ten cents into my hand and we went to the Salvation Army that night. She was very deaf and got me away up to the front. The Spirit of God took hold of me, and the Salvation Army people, in the way they have, got after me. One of the officers came up and said, 'Are you saved?' I said, 'No, I could not be saved.' I managed to get out of the meeting that night without giving my heart to God. But all the time there was something taking hold of me. I tried to drown it in drink. On Sunday night with the old lady I was back at the Army again. On Monday night I was drunk again. On Tuesday night I knelt down and gave my heart to Jesus, and a Salvationist said, 'Now brother, if you want the Lord to do anything, you just tell Him.'

"Before that time I had served two terms in the penitentiary. Sometimes twice a week I would be brought into the Police Court for drunkenness. Every time I went out and got drunk I would get arrested. I tried to get away from this life and went out West. I thought if I got out there and got into new surroundings things would be different. I got as far as Hornsville, New York, and got arrested there. I got a little further West and was arrested again. But I never got rid of the kind of life I used to live until I came to the Lord Jesus Christ. That was thirty years ago. The Lord is not only able to save a man but, thank God, He is able to keep him."

This is the story of an English baronet. He went wrong in England, came to America as a cow boy, was wild and reckless, but was soundly converted. He said: "I will not say much about myself. Perhaps you already know something about me. You may have seen my picture in the papers, telling of my past life, but I want to try to tell you, to the glory of God, how I was born again.

"When I succeeded my father to one of the oldest titles in England, in the year 1907, I was wild and reckless. I came over to America. To escape from a wild scrape I beat the sheriff in Colorado into Utah. Then I went home to England in 1908 and took over the title of the estate, and I made the occasion simply one drunken spree. I was out for all the devilment I could get into. I hated the Church. I hated religion. I hated anything good. When I went down to the old church which is in the grounds of the estate, they said to me, 'What will you do about the minister?' I said, 'I would kick the fool out, but the law would make me put in another.' If anybody mentioned the Salvation Army to me, I would refer to them as thieves and liars.

"I came back to America and immediately got involved in some more sprees, such as driving horses into saloons, and other devilment. Then I crossed again to London and started a wild-west show of my own in the London Hippodrome. I came back to America deeper in sin than ever. One day I was sitting in a saloon planning a fresh escapade when a Salvation Army sister came in with her tambourine and some 'War Cries.' She looked at me and said, 'Are you a Christian?' I said, 'No.' She gave me the address of the Headquarters and asked me to come up. The bar-tender turned round and said, 'Go up and rope somebody.' I said, 'I will go up.' There was something different about me. I did not know what was wrong with myself I went up to the open-air meeting and was as quiet as a mouse. For five or six days I could not keep away from the Headquarters. I did not know what was wrong. I went out to see some moving pictures to see if I could see myself amongst them; then I went and had another drink; but back to the Salvation Army Headquarters I had to go. I was getting almost crazy. I reached the point when I had either to give in or kill myself.

"I locked the door of my room and then got down on my knees and asked God to forgive me. Do you know, it seemed as if hell was turned loose around me. Everything said, 'You have gone too far; you are too big a sinner,' I said, 'But Jesus died for me.' I prayed and prayed, and I heard that voice come and say, 'Go and sin no more,' It was just as if a finger had touched my soul. My prayer turned from one of supplication to one of thankfulness for what God had done for me. I was born again. I rose up with the old life gone, and my two greatest blessings are that all that old life is blotted out for ever, and that I have the knowledge that the Spirit of Jesus my Saviour is in me, and I dwell in Him. The union between us is perfect. I thank God for that."

The following story was told by a man who had been a successful lawyer. He had gone down into the depths of sin and by the power of God's grace had been redeemed. He began by saying:--

Must Jesus bear the Cross alone,
And all the world go free?
No, there's a cross for you to bear,
And there's a cross for me.

"It is a cross for me to come here and relate my experience, but I am glad to be here inasmuch as something I say may gladden someone who is discouraged. I was brought up in a Christian home. My mother was a good woman and my father was a clergyman. I went through college and the lower school before I took a single drop of strong drink. But when I took my first drink--I remember it well--it seemed to be something I had been looking for all my life and had never found before. From that time on I drank periodically. I had a lovely family and an honoured name, but I dragged it and my family into the dust. I struggled through my own strength to redeem myself, but I could not, nor can any man. I took cures, but they availed me not. I was in the hospital fourteen times, struggling up all the time, but falling down again. I seemed too hopeless. The light seemed to be fading for ever from the horizon, and darkness was coming over me. I was without hope. I would rather have fallen asleep in death, away from my companions, away from my loved ones, and never have been seen again, than to have lived the way I was. But through the providence of God, and through a kind wife and sister, I am able to stand here to-day. God bless the wives of the drunkards and drinking men, for if any will have a crown in heaven, it will be the wife of the drunkard who stands by him through thick and thin and who never gives him up.

"I went away to a certain town and while there I noticed the title of a book called 'Twice Born Men.' It aroused my curiosity, and I picked it up and commenced to read it. I came to the story of the puncher, a man who was formerly a prize fighter, and who had descended to the lowest scale of humanity. He had become a drunkard of the worst type and had gone one night into a saloon with murder in his heart. He was going home to kill his wife, when there flashed in upon him some strange influence, some mighty influence, some compelling influence--the power of the Almighty--and drove him into the Salvation Army barracks, and there he knelt at the Penitent form and God took the load from his back. When he rose up there was a new light in his eyes, a new heart in his breast, and he arose a new born man. He began to work for Christ.

"As I read that story I said, 'If there is hope for the puncher, there is hope for me.' I had been brought up a Christian, and during my drinking days I had attended church, and I had fought as every poor drunkard fights to redeem himself. But through my own strength I failed, and I want to say to you here, there is no man who suffers pangs of bitter conscience or from a broken heart more than a poor drunkard who cannot tear the chains from himself. Have pity on him. And I read about this man going out to save those who were lost, and then I read on further about Danny, a drunkard, who while in prison was visited by the puncher, who sought him out, and said, 'There is a better life for you.' He took him to his home, and it was a new and happy home he took him to, with a happy wife and children, and he laboured with them. Danny the thief; Danny the drunkard; Danny the murderer. When the day had passed Danny went back to prison. But the power of God came over Danny in prison, and he said to himself, 'If God can save the puncher, God can save me.' And then there came into his heart a light; and I said, 'If God can save the puncher; if God can save Danny--He can save me.' And He did save me, and He has kept me, and from that day to this I have never desired a drop of alcohol.

"I have gone through physical sufferings that are attendant upon it, but thanks be unto God through the Lord Jesus Christ, He gave me the victory, and I stand here to-day an example of the keeping power of God. Oh, my friends, what a new life it opened up for me. I thought I was a Christian once; but until I was thrown down, until I was crucified twice over, not until then could I be convinced that God could save me from this terrible curse. And I want to say that no Christian man ever came to me and told me that God could save me from wrong. Oh, what a duty rests upon Christians to speak to the drinking men! When God took me by the hand I had a new life and I wanted to go out and save drunkards, and I have been trying to save them since. I went to the Salvation Army Barracks in Jersey City, and if it was not for the Salvation Army, I do not know whether I could have held out or not, but when I felt distressed those brothers prayed and stood round me, and if there is anyone here who is discouraged, and who is away from God, and who goes round the corner to see his little children going to school because he cannot go home, if there is anyone who has left a broken-hearted mother or wife at home; get up and go home to them and give your heart to the Lord."

The last story told at the meeting has to do with the complete transformation of a woman's life. It is a modern miracle. The one who tells the story is growing old and feeble, but all are thrilled as they listen to her.

This woman was educated in a young ladies' seminary, and had a fairly good start in life among some of the leading people in Western New York. She married a man who became an habitual drunkard. She was sorely disappointed in him, and, little by little, she started to drink, till there came the time when she and her husband were possibly two of the worst drunkards the State had ever known. She had been in prison two hundred or more times. But now, up in the little town of Canandaigua where she lives, she is treasurer of the Salvation Army, and has been for fifteen years. She is respected by all who know her. Not only the people in the army, but the well-to-do people of the town all love and respect Mary Law.

Her husband was not converted until recently. She had been praying fifteen years for him, and one night she prayed specially for him, the last half hour of the meeting passed, the last twenty minutes, and then Charlie came.

"I thank God for what He did for me," she said. "Before the Salvation Army got hold of me, I was one of the worst drunkards in the state of New York. The first night they came I wanted to know what the Salvation Army was like. Just like any other old drunken sot, I wanted to know what the Salvation Army was going to be. So I walked out as far as the Police Station, and I said, 'Where is the Salvation Army going to be to-night?' 'Well,' said the police officer, 'it is going to be up at the Presbyterian Church, but I want to tell you one thing. If you go up there you will get run in,' I thought to myself for a moment, if I stay out I will get run in, so I might just as well go up there and get run in. I went up, and I suppose I was a terrible-looking object. I got into a corner near the door, so that if anything turned up I could get out. I had just one quarter in my purse when they came to take up the collection, and I put that quarter in. I believe if I had been outside I would have been run in. When I got outside I wanted that quarter for a bottle of whisky. I then went up to the Police Station. When the Police Justice saw me coming in he said, 'Where have you been to-night?' I said, 'Up to the Salvation Army meeting.' 'Well,' he said, 'let me give you a little bit of advice. Keep right on going.'

"The first night they had their meeting in the hall I went to the penitent form, and the next night I got saved. That was over fifteen years ago. I have neither tasted nor handled one drop of intoxicating liquor from that day to this. I did not have a home fit for a dog to live in. I hardly ever knew what it was to be without a black eye. I have been pounded until I did not know where I was; until I was dazed. And when I came to, and saw where I was, I was lying on the floor and Charlie was lying on the bed with his dirty old clothes on, and if anybody has gone through hell, it is I. But I thank God to-day I have got just as good a husband as there is in the state of New York. I have just as comfortable a home as anybody could wish, and every dollar of it is paid for. Before that the saloons got the money, but I thank God to-day the saloons don't get any of my money.

"Charlie would get arrested, and when I saw him locked up, I would do something that would get me locked up too. We went in together and we came out together, We would not be out for long when back we would go again. If one went to the lock-up, the other went, and that is the way we carried on through life.

"An election campaign was being held many years ago, and Charlie went up the street to vote. He came home drunk. I suppose it was election whisky, but he brought some home, and we had a drink together. We went to bed on Tuesday night, and woke up intending to go to work the next day. I asked one of the neighbours what time it was, and she said it is almost night now, but where have you been for the last two or three days? We had gone to sleep on Tuesday night and did not wake up till Thursday night. I went back, and we took another drink that night, and did not wake up till Saturday night. If my life, sixteen years ago, was not hell upon earth, I do not know what you call hell.

"Just about the time when I first started out to serve God in Canandaigua, I was an outcast. Nobody cared for me. Nobody would notice me. When they saw me they would go out of their way to avoid me. Nobody wanted to come near me. But when I was drunk I thought I was about as good as they were, and sometimes I gave them a little of my mind, and that was the way I often got arrested. But to-day those very folks, who were my very worst enemies, who tried to hurt me and who did everything they could to injure me, are my very best friends. I have friends among the rich, and friends among the poor. They do not shun my home, they come and see me, and if I am sick some of the wealthy people come to see how I am getting along, and if I have everything I want. For all this I have to thank God and the Salvation Army.

"I have been kicked and knocked and pounded until I have been almost dead. Charlie did the kicking and the pounding, but I was as much to blame as he was. I was drunk and so was he, but I was never the one to go to the police officer and get a warrant out for my husband. If he pounded me until I could hardly breathe, and he happened to get arrested for it, I managed to get arrested too. I cannot tell you how many times we have been in jail in the little village of Elgin, and in the penitentiary too. But I would rather go back to the penitentiary to-day and spend my days there than to live again the life that I lived before I was converted. I thank God and the Salvation Army to-night that I do not have to carry black eyes, and that I can go home in peace.

"I have a nice comfortable home, and it is all paid for, and if it had not been for the Salvation Army coming to Canandaigua, I would have been in a drunkard's hell to-day. When the Army first came there, I was like a great many others. I wanted to see what the Salvation Army was like, and out of curiosity I went to a meeting. But I was too drunk to understand anything about it. The next night I went there quite sober, and I gave my heart to the Lord. That was seventeen years ago, and I thank God that since then I have tried to do my utmost to serve Him to the best of my ability. And it is my determination, as long as He gives me breath, to do for Him all I can, to spread His Kingdom on earth."

# CHAPTER XI
## *A Final Word*

As has been suggested, it is necessary, if one is to be a successful personal worker, to know well the Scriptures. The incorruptible seed, which is the Word of God, when it is received into the human heart as good and honest ground, will, without question, produce a satisfactory harvest. If you should attempt to win one to Christ, who insists that he is out of the Kingdom because of his doubts, tell him to come with his doubts, and Christ will set him free. "My doubts are round about me like a chain," said one in the audience, with whom one of our personal workers was labouring, and the worker said quickly, "Come, chains and all." The doubter hesitated a second, then said, "I will," and as he rose to move forward, he testified that the chains were snapped, and he was free.

If the one you are seeking to introduce to Christ says that he is such a great sinner, and because of this he cannot come, then tell him to come with his sins. He wants him just as he is, and stands ready to set him free from the sins that have enslaved him and blinded his eyes so that he could not see Christ as he stood waiting to save him.

It is a good thing to start by giving the assurance to the unsaved that God is Love, and that His love is boundless. This may be easily proved by the Scriptures. Tell him also that Christ is not only able, but ready and willing to save. There are abundant evidences of this in the New Testament. Tell him that no one is too sinful; none too far from God; none too depraved by sin to be saved. There are evidences on every side of us of many such seeking and finding pardon.

It is well to start with such a declaration as is found in John i. 12, "But as many as received Him, to them gave He power to become the sons of God, even to them that believe on His name." Insist upon it that Christ has laid down the conditions, and that if we are to be saved, we must honestly and sincerely, with all our doubts and sins, receive Him as a personal Saviour.

Make it very plain to the one with whom you are dealing that when one comes into the Kingdom he is born into it. There is no other way than this, for Jesus said, John iii. 3, "Except a man be born again he cannot see the Kingdom of God." If the joy of regeneration is to be experienced, it is necessary that the acceptance of Jesus as a Saviour should be definite, and that there should be sufficient confidence in God's Word to lead us to believe that when we have fulfilled our part of the contract the Saviour will keep His.

If we are born into the Kingdom then we start as babes in Christ. We are expected to grow. If we are to grow, we must have proper food; this is found in the Word of God. We must be faithful in prayer. We must have proper light and air;

this is found by walking in fellowship with Christ, and learning His will as we study the Scripture, we seek with joy to do it. We may stumble as little children do, but He will help us, and if at times we seem to fail, He will hold us fast.

As little babes in Christ it will not be strange that at times we grow discouraged and faint-hearted, but if we press on to know the Lord we shall find our strength increasing and our temptations decreasing until at last we may enter into a continuous and joyous Christian experience.

Tell the one with whom you are dealing that the assurance of salvation is possible. Jesus said, "He that heareth my word, and believeth on Him that sent Me, hath everlasting life, and shall not come into condemnation, but is passed from death unto life" (John v. 24). And the Apostle John wrote, "These things have I written unto you that believe on the name of the Son of God; that ye may know that ye have eternal life and that ye may believe on the name of the Son of God" (1 John v. 13).

State very plainly the fact that we are saved by faith and not by feeling, and being thus saved we are kept by Divine Power.

When we have passed through the darkness of doubt into the light of our conscious acceptance of Christ, and when on the authority of God's Word we have the assurance of salvation, then let it ever be remembered that we must seek to bring others to Him. And as we labour day by day our own faith will grow stronger, our hope will be brighter, and our consciousness of the presence of Christ will be more marked. Day by day we may walk with Him and talk with Him until at last we shall see Him as He is and then we may hear Him say, "Well done, good and faithful servant ... enter thou into the joy of thy Lord."

### The Codes Of Hammurabi And Moses
### W. W. Davies

QTY

The discovery of the Hammurabi Code is one of the greatest achievements of archaeology, and is of paramount interest, not only to the student of the Bible, but also to all those interested in ancient history...

**Religion**　　ISBN: *1-59462-338-4*　　　Pages:132

*MSRP $12.95*

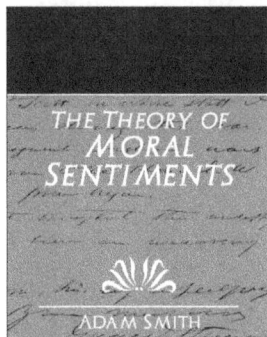

### The Theory of Moral Sentiments
### Adam Smith

QTY

This work from 1749. contains original theories of conscience amd moral judgment and it is the foundation for systemof morals.

**Philosophy**  ISBN: *1-59462-777-0*　　　Pages:536

*MSRP $19.95*

### Jessica's First Prayer
### Hesba Stretton

QTY

In a screened and secluded corner of one of the many railway-bridges which span the streets of London there could be seen a few years ago, from five o'clock every morning until half past eight, a tidily set-out coffee-stall, consisting of a trestle and board, upon which stood two large tin cans, with a small fire of charcoal burning under each so as to keep the coffee boiling during the early hours of the morning when the work-people were thronging into the city on their way to their daily toil...

**Childrens**　　ISBN: *1-59462-373-2*

Pages:84

*MSRP $9.95*

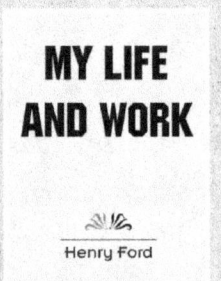

### My Life and Work
### Henry Ford

QTY

Henry Ford revolutionized the world with his implementation of mass production for the Model T automobile.  Gain valuable business insight into his life and work with his own auto-biography... "We have only started on our development of our country we have not as yet, with all our talk of wonderful progress, done more than scratch the surface. The progress has been wonderful enough but..."

**Biographies/**　　ISBN: *1-59462-198-5*

Pages:300

*MSRP $21.95*

## The Art of Cross-Examination
## Francis Wellman

QTY

I presume it is the experience of every author, after his first book is published upon an important subject, to be almost overwhelmed with a wealth of ideas and illustrations which could readily have been included in his book, and which to his own mind, at least, seem to make a second edition inevitable. Such certainly was the case with me; and when the first edition had reached its sixth impression in five months, I rejoiced to learn that it seemed to my publishers that the book had met with a sufficiently favorable reception to justify a second and considerably enlarged edition. ..

**Pages:412**

**Reference**   **ISBN: *1-59462-647-2***     *MSRP $19.95*

## On the Duty of Civil Disobedience
## Henry David Thoreau

QTY

Thoreau wrote his famous essay, On the Duty of Civil Disobedience, as a protest against an unjust but popular war and the immoral but popular institution of slave-owning. He did more than write—he declined to pay his taxes, and was hauled off to gaol in consequence. Who can say how much this refusal of his hastened the end of the war and of slavery ?

**Law**        **ISBN: *1-59462-747-9***        **Pages:48**

*MSRP $7.45*

## Dream Psychology Psychoanalysis for Beginners
## Sigmund Freud

QTY

Sigmund Freud, born Sigismund Schlomo Freud (May 6, 1856 - September 23, 1939), was a Jewish-Austrian neurologist and psychiatrist who co-founded the psychoanalytic school of psychology. Freud is best known for his theories of the unconscious mind, especially involving the mechanism of repression; his redefinition of sexual desire as mobile and directed towards a wide variety of objects; and his therapeutic techniques, especially his understanding of transference in the therapeutic relationship and the presumed value of dreams as sources of insight into unconscious desires.

**Pages:196**

**Psychology**   **ISBN: *1-59462-905-6***     *MSRP $15.45*

## The Miracle of Right Thought
## Orison Swett Marden

QTY

Believe with all of your heart that you will do what you were made to do. When the mind has once formed the habit of holding cheerful, happy, prosperous pictures, it will not be easy to form the opposite habit. It does not matter how improbable or how far away this realization may see, or how dark the prospects may be, if we visualize them as best we can, as vividly as possible, hold tenaciously to them and vigorously struggle to attain them, they will gradually become actualized, realized in the life. But a desire, a longing without endeavor, a yearning abandoned or held indifferently will vanish without realization.

**Pages:360**

**Self Help**       **ISBN: *1-59462-644-8***     *MSRP $25.45*

QTY

**The Rosicrucian Cosmo-Conception Mystic Christianity** *by Max Heindel*    ISBN: *1-59462-188-8*   **$38.95**
*The Rosicrucian Cosmo-conception is not dogmatic, neither does it appeal to any other authority than the reason of the student. It is: not controversial, but is: sent forth in the hope that it may help to clear...*
*New Age/Religion Pages 646*

**Abandonment To Divine Providence** *by Jean-Pierre de Caussade*    ISBN: *1-59462-228-0*   **$25.95**
*"The Rev. Jean Pierre de Caussade was one of the most remarkable spiritual writers of the Society of Jesus in France in the 18th Century. His death took place at Toulouse in 1751. His works have gone through many editions and have been republished...*
*Inspirational/Religion Pages 400*

**Mental Chemistry** *by Charles Haanel*    ISBN: *1-59462-192-6*   **$23.95**
*Mental Chemistry allows the change of material conditions by combining and appropriately utilizing the power of the mind. Much like applied chemistry creates something new and unique out of careful combinations of chemicals the mastery of mental chemistry...*
*New Age Pages 354*

**The Letters of Robert Browning and Elizabeth Barret Barrett 1845-1846 vol II**    ISBN: *1-59462-193-4*   **$35.95**
*by Robert Browning and Elizabeth Barrett*
*Biographies Pages 596*

**Gleanings In Genesis (volume I)** *by Arthur W. Pink*    ISBN: *1-59462-130-6*   **$27.45**
*Appropriately has Genesis been termed "the seed plot of the Bible" for in it we have, in germ form, almost all of the great doctrines which are afterwards fully developed in the books of Scripture which follow...*
*Religion/Inspirational Pages 420*

**The Master Key** *by L. W. de Laurence*    ISBN: *1-59462-001-6*   **$30.95**
*In no branch of human knowledge has there been a more lively increase of the spirit of research during the past few years than in the study of Psychology, Concentration and Mental Discipline. The requests for authentic lessons in Thought Control, Mental Discipline and...*
*New Age/Business Pages 422*

**The Lesser Key Of Solomon Goetia** *by L. W. de Laurence*    ISBN: *1-59462-092-X*   **$9.95**
*This translation of the first book of the "Lemegton" which is here for the first time made accessible to students of Talismanic Magic was done, after careful collation and edition, from numerous Ancient Manuscripts in Hebrew, Latin, and French...*
*New Age/Occult Pages 92*

**Rubaiyat Of Omar Khayyam** *by Edward Fitzgerald*    ISBN:*1-59462-332-5*   **$13.95**
*Edward Fitzgerald, whom the world has already learned, in spite of his own efforts to remain within the shadow of anonymity, to look upon as one of the rarest poets of the century, was born at Bredfield, in Suffolk, on the 31st of March, 1809. He was the third son of John Purcell...*
*Music Pages 172*

**Ancient Law** *by Henry Maine*    ISBN: *1-59462-128-4*   **$29.95**
*The chief object of the following pages is to indicate some of the earliest ideas of mankind, as they are reflected in Ancient Law, and to point out the relation of those ideas to modern thought.*
*Religiom/History Pages 452*

**Far-Away Stories** *by William J. Locke*    ISBN: *1-59462-129-2*   **$19.45**
*"Good wine needs no bush, but a collection of mixed vintages does. And this book is just such a collection. Some of the stories I do not want to remain buried for ever in the museum files of dead magazine-numbers an author's not unpardonable vanity..."*
*Fiction Pages 272*

**Life of David Crockett** *by David Crockett*    ISBN: *1-59462-250-7*   **$27.45**
*"Colonel David Crockett was one of the most remarkable men of the times in which he lived. Born in humble life, but gifted with a strong will, an indomitable courage, and unremitting perseverance...*
*Biographies/New Age Pages 424*

**Lip-Reading** *by Edward Nitchie*    ISBN: *1-59462-206-X*   **$25.95**
*Edward B. Nitchie, founder of the New York School for the Hard of Hearing, now the Nitchie School of Lip-Reading, Inc, wrote "LIP-READING Principles and Practice". The development and perfecting of this meritorious work on lip-reading was an undertaking...*
*How-to Pages 400*

**A Handbook of Suggestive Therapeutics, Applied Hypnotism, Psychic Science**    ISBN: *1-59462-214-0*   **$24.95**
*by Henry Munro*
*Health/New Age/Health/Self-help Pages 376*

**A Doll's House: and Two Other Plays** *by Henrik Ibsen*    ISBN: *1-59462-112-8*   **$19.95**
*Henrik Ibsen created this classic when in revolutionary 1848 Rome. Introducing some striking concepts in playwriting for the realist genre, this play has been studied the world over.*
*Fiction/Classics/Plays 308*

**The Light of Asia** *by sir Edwin Arnold*    ISBN: *1-59462-204-3*   **$13.95**
*In this poetic masterpiece, Edwin Arnold describes the life and teachings of Buddha. The man who was to become known as Buddha to the world was born as Prince Gautama of India but he rejected the worldly riches and abandoned the reigns of power when...*
*Religion/History/Biographies Pages 170*

**The Complete Works of Guy de Maupassant** *by Guy de Maupassant*    ISBN: *1-59462-157-8*   **$16.95**
*"For days and days, nights and nights, I had dreamed of that first kiss which was to consecrate our engagement, and I knew not on what spot I should put my lips..."*
*Fiction/Classics Pages 240*

**The Art of Cross-Examination** *by Francis L. Wellman*    ISBN: *1-59462-309-0*   **$26.95**
*Written by a renowned trial lawyer, Wellman imparts his experience and uses case studies to explain how to use psychology to extract desired information through questioning.*
*How-to/Science/Reference Pages 408*

**Answered or Unanswered?** *by Louisa Vaughan*    ISBN: *1-59462-248-5*   **$10.95**
*Miracles of Faith in China*
*Religion Pages 112*

**The Edinburgh Lectures on Mental Science (1909)** *by Thomas*    ISBN: *1-59462-008-3*   **$11.95**
*This book contains the substance of a course of lectures recently given by the writer in the Queen Street Hail, Edinburgh. Its purpose is to indicate the Natural Principles governing the relation between Mental Action and Material Conditions...*
*New Age/Psychology Pages 148*

**Ayesha** *by H. Rider Haggard*    ISBN: *1-59462-301-5*   **$24.95**
*Verily and indeed it is the unexpected that happens! Probably if there was one person upon the earth from whom the Editor of this, and of a certain previous history, did not expect to hear again...*
*Classics Pages 380*

**Ayala's Angel** *by Anthony Trollope*    ISBN: *1-59462-352-X*   **$29.95**
*The two girls were both pretty, but Lucy who was twenty-one who supposed to be simple and comparatively unattractive, whereas Ayala was credited, as her Bombwhat romantic might show, with poetic charm and a taste for romance. Ayala when her father died was nineteen...*
*Fiction Pages 484*

**The American Commonwealth** *by James Bryce*    ISBN: *1-59462-286-8*   **$34.45**
*An interpretation of American democratic political theory. It examines political mechanics and society from the perspective of Scotsman James Bryce*
*Politics Pages 572*

**Stories of the Pilgrims** *by Margaret P. Pumphrey*    ISBN: *1-59462-116-0*   **$17.95**
*This book explores pilgrims religious oppression in England as well as their escape to Holland and eventual crossing to America on the Mayflower, and their early days in New England...*
*History Pages 268*

QTY

**The Fasting Cure** *by Sinclair Upton*                                                   ISBN: *1-59462-222-1*   **$13.95**
*In the Cosmopolitan Magazine for May, 1910, and in the Contemporary Review (London) for April, 1910, I published an article dealing with my experi-
ences in fasting. I have written a great many magazine articles, but never one which attracted so much attention...  New Age/Self Help/Health Pages 164*

**Hebrew Astrology** *by Sepharial*                                                        ISBN: *1-59462-308-2*   **$13.45**
*In these days of advanced thinking it is a matter of common observation that we have left many of the old landmarks behind and that we are now pressing
forward to greater heights and to a wider horizon than that which represented the mind-content of our progenitors...          Astrology Pages 144*

**Thought Vibration or The Law of Attraction in the Thought World**        ISBN: *1-59462-127-6*   **$12.95**
*by William Walker Atkinson*                                                            *Psychology/Religion Pages 144*

**Optimism** *by Helen Keller*                                                             ISBN: *1-59462-108-X*   **$15.95**
*Helen Keller was blind, deaf, and mute since 19 months old, yet famously learned how to overcome these handicaps, communicate with the world, and
spread her lectures promoting optimism.  An inspiring read for everyone...          Biographies/Inspirational Pages 84*

**Sara Crewe** *by Frances Burnett*                                                       ISBN: *1-59462-360-0*    **$9.45**
*In the first place, Miss Minchin lived in London. Her home was a large, dull, tall one, in a large, dull square, where all the houses were alike, and all the
sparrows were alike, and where all the door-knockers made the same heavy sound...          Childrens/Classic Pages 88*

**The Autobiography of Benjamin Franklin** *by Benjamin Franklin*           ISBN: *1-59462-135-7*   **$24.95**
*The Autobiography of Benjamin Franklin has probably been more extensively read than any other American historical work, and no other book of its kind
has had such ups and downs of fortune. Franklin lived for many years in England, where he was agent...          Biographies/History Pages 332*

| Name | |
|---|---|
| Email | |
| Telephone | |
| Address | |
| | |
| City, State ZIP | |

☐ **Credit Card**          ☐ **Check / Money Order**

| Credit Card Number | |
|---|---|
| Expiration Date | |
| Signature | |

*Please Mail to:*   Book Jungle
                          *PO Box 2226
                          Champaign, IL 61825*
        *or Fax to:*           *630-214-0564*

## ORDERING INFORMATION

**web***: www.bookjungle.com*
**email***: sales@bookjungle.com*
**fax***: 630-214-0564*
**mail***: Book Jungle  PO Box 2226  Champaign, IL 61825*
**or PayPal** *to sales@bookjungle.com*

*Please contact us for bulk discounts*

## DIRECT-ORDER TERMS

**20% Discount if You Order
Two or More Books**
Free Domestic Shipping!
Accepted: Master Card, Visa,
Discover, American Express

www.ingramcontent.com/pod-product-compliance
Lightning Source LLC
Chambersburg PA
CBHW081148170626
46809CB00010B/3139